THE QUADRILLE

MX Publishing

Other books in the CODE NAME DELTA series:

THE SECRET FILE OF PATRICK COONAN

THE QUADRILLE

Oscar Ortiz

MX Publishing

Book #1 in the CODE NAME DELTA series

To my son Alex Francisco,
my dear 'Big Guy'.

Praise for The Quadrille

AWARDED 5 STARS BY THE ONLINE BOOK CLUB

"The Quadrille, *by Oscar Ortiz, is an enthralling American action thriller set during the Cold War's final decades. The plot revolves around Sergeant Patrick Coonan, a ranger sniper recruited into the Quadrille, a covert unit tasked with thwarting Soviet 'dirty bomb' threats. The narrative captivates with Coonan's character development, showcasing his humanity amidst his lethal skills. Ortiz skillfully structures the story with well-defined chapters and character introductions. Coonan emerges as a standout hero, with his patriotism and wit endearing him to the readers. The book's flawless editing enhances the reading experience, earning it a perfect 5 out of 5 stars. Overall,* The Quadrille *delivers a gripping blend of action, espionage, and thriller elements, making it a must-read for fans of the genre.*

— **Ebere Writes Cocept**
Reviewed for The Online Book Club

THE FORGING OF AN AMERICAN ASSASSIN

"In his novel The Quadrille, *Oscar Ortiz plunges us into the underworld of clandestine state-sanctioned undertakings during the Cold War period. Thus, we witness the forging of an American assassin with a license to kill, from his recruitment to his deadly secret actions, after going through training. As if he somehow knows this environment much more than the ordinary citizen, Ortiz describes a credible process of creating a human killing machine while revealing an alleged terrorist plot by the former Soviet Union to bring the United States to its knees. What is most interesting are the so-called 'dirty methods' which are revealed as we follow*

in the footsteps of Agent Patrick Coonan, codenamed Delta. The usage of first-person narrative and the terrible murderous conspiracy Coonan faces, make us empathize with someone who is nothing more than an "eliminator," and therein lies one of Ortiz's greatest achievements in this work. The rampant action and certain other resources the author employs, make the reader get under the assassin's skin and into his mind, thus coming to believe that the actions of enforcers of this kind are not only necessary, but could even have a moral justification."

— **Rodolfo Pérez Valero**
5 times Winner of the "Noir Week Award" of Gijon, Spain

A TOPIC MANY HAVE CHOSEN TO IGNORE

"I have followed Oscar Ortiz's literary work in its various genres since the beginning. I believe that the CODE NAME DELTA series is among his best achievements and, after carefully reading its first installment, I consider it the door through which the readers will enter an interesting world through a tense plot, of incessant interest, sprinkled with anecdotes that will serve as refreshing pauses for a topic that many have preferred to ignore."

— **Leonel Rodríguez de la Torre**
New York & New Jersey-based Investigative Reporter

"Mors certa, hora incerta."

ACKNOWLEGMENT

My deepest thanks to Mr. Randall Masteller of *Spy Guys & Gals* for catching me in an unforgivable error. I had originally envisioned Patrick Coonan as a 24-year-old "young Sergeant Major" in the Ranger Corps. Having served for 12 years in our armed forces, Mr. Masteller made me aware that to reach said rank – in the U.S. Army – is far from possible at that age... Well, sorry, Pat, or should I call you Sergeant (E5) Coonan?

The Author

TABLE OF CONTENTS

FOREWORD

(An introduction to The Secret File of Patrick Coonan)

In recent times, the cinematic James Bond has been converted into a "catwalk muscleman" bearing an asphalt face and a propensity for melancholy. To escape from this new "politically correct" version of the character, incapable of being seductive and without any trace of the model developed by Ian Fleming in his novels, there still are few options available. The most obvious one is to review Fleming's books or the films starring Sean Connery and his most popular successors. Another option is the pulp narrative alternative to 007, currently well served by the prolific Cuban American writer Oscar Ortiz. This is the series *Code name Delta*, starring Patrick Coonan, a U.S. Rangers' sniper transformed into a clandestine operator for the Quadrille — the sharp Counterintelligence unit created by Ret. Special Forces Col. Marlon Berkowitz to safeguard America from all threats. Always with the protracted shadow of the Cold War as the background, which also served as the main setting in the first Bond book written by Fleming. Ortiz's virtues as a novelist can be well appreciated in all his Patrick Coonan adventures: a concise, direct prose, halfway between the Noir Mystery genre and the Spy thriller; utmost erudition in the different topics dealt with, where one perceives a thorough work of research and the offering to the reader of varied plots that combine investigation, violent death, sexuality, and an uncomfortable background of moral sordidness.

Josep Ferran Valls
Valencia, Spain - Oct. 2022

DRAMATIS PERSONAE

BALMASEDA (Leo)
A Manhattan-based P.I. of shady reputation. Many things are rumored about him, most of which are not very favorable. A tough guy, originally from the Bronx, who now lives and works in Jackson Heights, with connections in Manhattan's underworld.

BERKOWITZ (Marlon)
Alias "the Colonel," a former U.S. Special Forces colonel now retired. He is a veteran of the Vietnam War and the most recent invasion of Grenada. Col. Berkowitz is chosen by the DOD to recruit and shape a very special unit of covert operatives to eliminate Soviet Bloc saboteurs operating in the United States. He is the director of operations of the Quadrille, and Patrick Coonan's boss.

BYERS (Richard)
A.k.a. "Hippy Rick." An American Vietnam vet now turned soldier of fortune — friends with Mack — who is driven by drug and alcohol abuse, thus becoming an undesirable entity.

COONAN (Patrick)
Alias Delta. A young sergeant with the U.S. Ranger Corps, and an expert marksman who fought in Grenada performing covert missions assigned to him by Col. Berkowitz without Coonan's knowing. At the end of the conflict, he is stationed at Fort Benning, Georgia under Commander Silas Manor, and employed as master-instructor in the Rangers Sniper School.

DEMPSEY (Mack)
Alias "Candy Mack." An American hoodlum of Irish ancestry now turned mercenary — friends with "Hippy Rick" and "Black Lucas" —, also a Vietnam veteran. Mack belongs to the underworld fauna of Hell's Kitchen. Maintains shady business ties with P.I. Leo.

FURIAS (Emilio)
An "illegal agent" of the Cuban *Directorio General de Inteligencia* planted in Manhattan. He is friends with Mirta Velasco, and a former colleague of hers from their days with DGI's America Department. Emilio is an expert in martial arts, and very knowledgeable in spy craft techniques, such as

shadowing and photographing enemy agents from a distance.

JACKSON (Lucas)
A.k.a. "Black Lucas," he is an African American mercenary friend of Mack. Also, a Vietnam vet with connections in the Harlem underworld.

KIROV (Anatoli)
A full major in the Soviet KGB. Responsible for handling secret overseas operations entrusted to the Atomic Fang Division, an elite group of saboteurs operated by the feared *Komitet Gosudarstvennoy Bezopasnosti*.

KODINA (Andrei)
Chief of staff of the Atomic Fang Division of the KGB, operates under the exclusive command of Major Kirov.

MANOR (Silas)
A commander in the U.S. Army Ranger Corps. He oversees the Rangers Sniper School. He is the highest-ranking officer at Fort Benning, Georgia.

PAVENKO (Yuri)
An "illegal agent" of the Soviet KGB operating in New York. Yuri is one of the classified as "sleepers" for having spent many years living in the enemy camp. Considered by his superiors as the best saboteur in the entire Atomic Fang Division. He has an apartment in Queens but is also a regular in Manhattan's Latin salsa discos. Yuri has made a name for himself as a hedonist and womanizer, and a lover of the Latin American culture, music, and women.

TILSON (Alfred)
Former CIA agent, Alfred Tilson is a native of Boston. He is also a master-assassin stationed for almost 10 years at the CIA's Moscow Section. Tilson is brought by Col. Berkowitz to the Quadrille to train new recruits in the art of "the fifth profession" and thus forge the most efficient "wet works" unit in the entire American Counterintelligence community.

VELASCO (Mirta)
Cuban by birth, she infiltrates the U.S. through the Mariel Flotilla incident during Jimmy Carter's administration. Mirta is a former agent of the Cuban DGI, who now works as an "illegal" for the KGB. She is Yuri Pavenko's collaborator in the sabotage mission being carried out by the Atomic Fang Division in Manhattan.

P*rologue*

$\mathbf{D}$uring the last two decades of the Cold War, the Warsaw Pact nations with Soviet Russia in the vanguard, amassed a formidable array of armored divisions centered in Poland and the Czech Republic, close to the West German border. Concerned about the alarming balance of power, NATO's High Command estimated that it would take the Red Army and its allies just twenty-four hours to complete the invasion of Western Europe. The American response to this threat was to deploy a cordon of *Pershing II* missiles in the Federal Republic of Germany. After their placement, the first rockets were armed with nuclear warheads and aimed directly at the heart of Russia.

*C*hapter 1

TRIAL BY FIRE

My name is Patrick Coonan, but in the trade, I'm known as Agent Delta. For quite some years I operated as an "eliminator" under Col. Marlon Berkowitz's command, becoming a clandestine operative with a license to kill. But, before I begin my story, I'd like to clarify that the main motive that prompted me to make this underrated occupation my own was due to a woman's lack of love. Her name: Elizabeth Kelly.

Liz and I grew up in the same neighborhood, but it wasn't until high school that I noticed her. It took me around twelve months to work up the courage to court her, and finally declare my love to her. She had no qualms about accepting me as her boyfriend, and, for a while, I was the happiest man on earth. The problems began after several failed attempts, when I realized that it would not be possible to make her my woman until we were properly married; that's what her parents always demanded at the time. So, at the age of nineteen, I asked her to marry me.

For this special moment, I chose our high school graduation gala. And though I always saw her through the dreamful eyes of a love-struck moron, I had sensed in her an aloof frigidity that at times irritated me and became a crisis the moment I announced my intention to take her as my wife. Her categorical refusal came as a surprise.

"I'm sorry, Pat," she said showing no emotion, "but marriage is not in my plans for the time being. I'm getting ready for college."

Those indolent words still echo inside my cranial vault like shots fired at close range from a heavy-caliber gun. And even though I intended to take her rejection in good spirits, the truth is that my life was shattered. Nevertheless, it's not practical to cling to someone who doesn't share our goals and emotions; one must smile at the world and, even if you don't want to, take the blow as best we can and get back on track, right?

Well, that's what I did.

My restless and adventurous nature led me onto other paths that had little or nothing to do with academia, commerce, industry, and technology. Dad had been a police officer, and I didn't hesitate to follow in his footsteps, but my love for hunting in the mountains and the outdoors life tipped the scales in favor of the Army. So, after passing boot camp, I chose to join the Ranger Corps and become a sniper. My trial by fire took place in the invasion of Grenada, during Operation Urgent Fury, where I carried out — successfully, I might add — eleven secret assignments.

But that was back in October of 1983 and little did I know then that *this* was just the beginning!

*C*hapter **2**

THE ATOMIC FANG

When the news of our missile deployment in Europe spread, the Kremlin's reaction was immediate and brutal. Ipso facto, the Soviet regime's top security officials were instructed to come up with an emergency plan to respond to a nuclear attack, and the KGB's Atomic Fang Division was activated. Under said name operated a special task force of Russian saboteurs who infiltrated every major American coastal city. Their mission was to smuggle in portable atomic mines —also known as "dirty bombs" — and wait in the shadows for the detonation order.

I learned all this because once the Kremlin put its plan into action, I was recruited to stop them at all costs. A new Republican president was now in the White House, and the moments of cowardice and indecision that marked Jimmy Carter's administration were finally behind us, even if those debilitating misconceptions in U.S. foreign policy persisted, and continued to affect our nation's armed forces, denting our patriotic fervor and the old American fighting spirit.

But for all that, the enemy would soon learn that there were still people in our country who did not fear the fury of the Soviet bear. All it took on our part was a retired Special Forces colonel and a concise group of hand-picked shadow warriors who did not hesitate to get blood on their hands or put their necks on the line for God and Country.

We did what we did to ensure our future generations that the United States of America, as a fully democratic and sovereign nation, would retain its status as the world's first superpower for many years to come.

Thus, the Quadrille was born.

In Central Moscow, across Lubyanka Square, stands a massive structure covered in ochre-colored paint; its architectural features correspond to the Neo-Baroque style. The exact address of this stronghold is No. 2 Lubyanka Ploshchad, but almost everyone in Moscow calls it the Great Lubyanka Building. I remember reading somewhere that it was originally built as the head office of a Russian insurance agency. I never understood why it ended up being the KGB head-quarters. When the Bolshevik Revolution triumphed, the building was confiscated by the Communists for purposes far more sinister than selling insurance policies. They converted it into the operations center of a secret police force that saw more state-sanctioned torture and shootings than any other prison of its kind around the world.

It was at the end of 1983 that the events that would escalate the Cold War during this last period of its duration precipitated. The first upsurge in the conflict between the superpowers had taken place during the

October Crisis, almost two decades before, when Nikita Khrushchev and the Politburo gang made the decision to deploy atomic missiles in the nearby nation-island of Cuba. But on this occasion, the order issued by the Soviet Supreme fell like a hot potato on Maj. Anatoly Kirov's desk. Kirov was one of the veteran officers of Directorate S, and while he paced back and forth in his office, both hands well-clasped behind his back, the major reflected deeply about the issue. It was no small matter, mind you. For a moment, he paused to contemplate his workplace, then there was the sound of knuckles striking wood. Kirov looked towards the door and smiled. He knew the identity of the mysterious character calling at his door.

As Maj. Kirov summoned in the caller, the door opened and Andrei Kodina, a tall, half-bald, cadaverous-looking man stepped in. He wore thick myopic glasses and was dressed in a charcoal gray suit; the bottom of his pants too long, the excess fabric wrapped around his ankles. The red tie with the gold pin that identified him as a member of the Communist Party was not missing.

"Take a seat, comrade Chief of Staff."

The newcomer, who eyed Maj. Kirov with a certain air of reserve, was none other than the feared head of the Atomic Fang Division — let's call it AFD for short. However, for all his tough guy fame, Andrei Kodina humbly nodded and closed the door behind him as he rushed to obey the redoubtable Kirov's order.

"Thank you, Comrade Major." He mumbled quietly.

Anatoli Kirov sat behind his desk and pulled out a fresh pack of Russian cigarettes from a drawer, the packet was wrapped in soft pastel-colored paper. He took one out and placed it carefully between his lips without offering the visitor, then he touched the tip of the ciggy to the flame of a heavy table lighter that might have been made of copper, or bronze. After blowing his first puff of smoke, the major ceremoniously grabbed the silver teapot resting on the desk by the handle and poured the steaming beverage into a matching pair of fine porcelain cups. One of them was pushed towards the man over the burnished surface of the desk. Pausing for dramatic effect, Kirov took a moment to contemplate his desk before speaking. Months later, observing the scene through the scope of a long-range rifle, I realized that this was a ritual the KGB officer often practiced when absorbed in one of his brainstorms.

The surrounding room was vast and adorned with heavy mahogany-and-leather furniture, as well as ostentatious portraits of present and past Soviet leaders. On display were photos of Feliks Dzerzhinsky, the late comrade leader Leonid Brezhnev, and the current leader of the Communist Party of the USSR, supreme commander of the entire Soviet Union, Yuri Andropov.

Dzerzhinsky — I was informed of this later, during the preliminary phase of my training — was a bloodthirsty Pole, an atheist, who founded the KGB under the name CHEKA before it became the NKGB, then the MGB before 1954, when it was officially reorganized as the *Komitet Gosudarstvennoy Bezopasnosti*. But only the name of the organization changed, and I suppose it did so for political reasons, because the essence of its functions never evolved.

Since its inception, the KGB has always been a body

attached to the Council of Ministers responsible for internal security, gathering both foreign and domestic intelligence and acting as secret police. You can picture it as the equivalent of our CIA, combined with the FBI, the Border Patrol, and the National Security Agency, merging the four agencies into one colossal institution, with the National Guard also under its command thrown in for good measure. Anyway, it's worth noting that it was made up of a constellation of departments, starting with the First Directorate of Operations (Foreign Intelligence), followed by the Second Directorate (Internal Security and Counterespionage), the Eighth Directorate (Encryption and Government Communications) and numerous other branches, culminating in the Border Guard. Twenty sections in all, each with a different undertaking. Get the picture?

Finally, Maj. Kirov took a sip from his tea and a drag on his cigarette. "I have a question for you, comrade", he spoke grimly, "and I beg you to take your time to answer it...."

Again, he paused for maximum effect before voicing the inquiry: "Who do you consider the best saboteur in the entire Atomic Fang Division?"

Chapter 3

A MESSAGE FROM ABROAD

On Christmas Eve, a few days before the start of the New Year's festivities, a man named Yuri Pavenko made a name for himself at a Latin salsa disco in Manhattan. The hands of the clock were almost striking midnight, but the place, which had been open since Happy Hour, was packed with enthusiastic salsa music lovers, many of them bustling around the 30-meter-long pure marble bar counter. Others were seated at the tables lining the dance floor.

The resonant melody broadcasted by a high-fidelity sound system was deafening, but Pavenko did not seem bothered in the slightest — which was odd, right? A Slav is not exactly the sort of person to fit in at such a boisterous place, occupied mainly by Caribs and Hispanics. But the Russian was enjoying himself in this exotic, colorful ambiance, leaning against the bar drumming with fingers as thick as Polish sausages on the marble top; he was following the rhythms of the Fania All-Stars. The band's lead vocalist sang a song, perfectly replicating Héctor Lavoe's voice, with the same drunken accent and exaggerated nasal tone that would make the Puerto Rican singer famous.

Pavenko ordered a drink. He was perched on the far right of the bar, a strategic position for those who did not want to miss anything happening on the dance floor, even if hunting femmes was easier at the other end.

The Russian was not very tall, but he was corpulent, with a blatant tendency towards obesity; his body was not flabby, but solid, with a broad back topped by powerful shoulders. His straight, wheat-colored hair was neatly trimmed, as were his mustache and goatee. His hawk-like brow, and a short, aquiline nasal appendage, broke the roundness with which a double jowl wedged his face. His dossier indicated that he was five feet ten inches tall and weighed roughly two hundred and thirty pounds; his general appearance was that of a wine barrel in full regalia.

From a side pocket of his coat, Pavenko extracted a pack of red and gold Dunhill cigarettes; like the hedonist he was, he smoked only English ciggies. He lit one with a gold-plated Ronson, before propping his butt on a swiveling barstool to enjoy the show. He was in the process of doing so when an attractive female specimen in her thirties, with long jet-black hair, left her chair at one of the tables near the dance floor and hurried towards the lounge's exit. On the way, the woman pretended she was compelled to pass by the bar.

She stopped for a moment in front of the Russian, as if suddenly recognizing him, and forcing a mellow smile approached him.

"Hello, Yuri! Thought I recognized you...." She addressed him in heavily accented English. Hers was a strong Spanish accent.

Pavenko grinned in turn and let his mischievous little eyes roam up and down the woman's superb anatomy; he made no attempt to conceal his lust. She was wearing a red satin dress that clung to her body like a second skin. Opulent curves, shapely legs, a narrow waist, and a remarkable derriere that betrayed her African ancestry. To top it all off, there was the light caramel tone of her silky skin and the lush red lips that drove the Russian spy crazy.

Pavenko knew her background well, of course, he knew she had been born in Cuba but now resided in The States and that her full name was Mirta Alicia Velasco. Although to tell the truth — judging by the photos of her he'd found in her file — when she'd arrived on the Mariel Flotilla three years earlier, she hadn't looked as good as she did now... *Ah*, he thought with thrilling irony, *the miracles of Capitalism!*

"Mirta, baby! What a pleasure to see you, girl; you just arrived?"

His voice was husky, like a caveman's; his English almost perfect and with the same accent as us gringos, not that British English you are taught in Europe and some Latin American countries. But, of course, this was to be expected, given that he was an illegal agent of the KGB's Directorate S, operating on American soil.

"Actually, I'm leaving; I'm very tired." Replied the Cuban. "But I'm happy to see you, big guy; maybe another time...."

Flashing a seductive smile, she moved closer to him and spread out her arms to embrace him. While the Russian held her close to his body, Mirta took the opportunity to slip a folded piece of paper into one of his coat pockets. Nobody noticed. She allowed Pavenko's hands to caress her curves, even felt the birth of an erection under his clothes, but the message had already been delivered and so she disengaged herself from him and turned towards the exit. Pavenko followed her with sinful eyes until the Cuban disappeared; only then did he plunge his right hand into the pregnant pocket and pull out the folded piece of paper that hadn't been there before.

He carefully unfolded it and checked the missive printed in Cyrillic. It read something like this:

FOR YOUR EYES ONLY: A module is on the way... It has been broken down into six components... It will arrive by sea, and each element has been scheduled to reach you on the first of the month... Make the arrangement for pick-ups.

*C*hapter *4*

THE COLONEL

I would not find out about all that was going on in our own backyard until a few weeks later, once I got stationed in Fort Benning, Georgia. Operation Urgent Fury had come to an end, and the U.S. Army gave the order to extract me from the island of Grenada, and ship me back to The States without pomp, I should clarify, because though I came to be considered a hero in certain circles at that time — after having successfully completed quite a few missions as a sniper — it is no less true that it was a heroism of incognito. As no other armed conflicts were anticipated in which to employ me in the near future, the fort commander decided to use my proficiency as an expert marksman to train the new recruits entering the Ranger Corps Sniper School. His name was Silas Manor: a cagey black man of Herculean dimensions, with a heart of gold and a lot more patriotism than good old George Washington himself. He would be the first to realize that the course of my life was about to change.

The unexpected call reached Commander Manor's office one cold morning in early January 1984. The multi-line telephone on his desk began to ring. I could almost hear it from the shooting range below, my vantage point; I could also contemplate Silas Manor's massive profile silhouetted against the window frame of his second story workplace. He had taken to watching me as I endeavored to show my class how the Haskins long-range rifle was dismantled and reassembled in less than a minute.

At the insistent ringing of the phone, the commanding officer of the fort stepped away from the window and went to *sit* down on the swivel chair behind his desk to take the call.

"Commander Manor," he growled into the headset, listening to the voice on the other end of the line. "Who do you say, Col. Berkowitz from Washington, D.C.? Sure, I'll take the call."

The next thing I knew, an MP showed up at the barracks asking for Sergeant Coonan. This happened late one evening when I had decided to tuck myself in early, since the following day promised to be long and exhausting. The shooting tests that were being conducted with two new battalions of recruits were not something I was looking forward to; trust me. I noticed the first symptom of anomaly in the energetic attitude of the gorilla they sent to get me. This MP was huge and behaved like a jerk; he defecated on my sergeant's stripes, petulantly ordering me to dress up quickly and to follow him out to the camp. I remember that he was packing a .45 semiauto in a shiny hip holster and held an M-16 assault rifle in his arms; his body language made it clear that he was ready to use them, should I decide to give him any trouble.

Once fully dressed in combat uniform, I was led to one end of the camp, and it didn't take me long to realize where he was escorting me. It also took me by surprise, since at no time had I heard any rumors of war. We went straight to some sort of shack built with wooden boards and corrugated metal, the place we called The Hut. There was nothing special about the dwelling, except that it was the rendezvous point chosen by the barracks strategists in charge of assigning all the secret missions.

I entered the shack without asking my escort any dumb questions for which this man would have no answers. It wasn't the first time, mind you, that I'd been involved in a similar situation. Once I went in, the MP shut the door behind me and stood guard outside.

The interior of The Hut resembled an office of sorts, with panels of faux wood covering the walls, a large desk with two chairs in the very center of the room, and five metal filing cabinets lined up against the far wall. Sitting behind the desk was a white male in his mid-forties with a clean-shaven head and near-sighted glasses. He was dressed in civilian clothes with a Brook Brothers suit and looked like a stockbroker or a banker, but, to a good observer, his military poise betrayed itself in the way he carried himself. He didn't fool me one bit; the strong sangfroid radiating from his personality suggested that the gent in question was one of those men with bars and stripes on his shoulders. His angular face was inlaid in a thick file, which he seemed to read while chewing on the stem of a briar pipe he kept unlit.

I watched everything intently, but kept my mouth shut until the man raised his eyes to stare at me.

"Evening, Sgt. Coonan."

"Good evening, sir" I responded, there would be no chevrons visible on his shoulders but in the military the first thing you are taught is to always show respect — even if you wish otherwise.

"You can call me *sir,* or you can call me *colonel*; I no longer wear the uniform of the Armed Forces, but I still pull the rank. I prefer not to use names for now. Do you agree?"

"Yes, sir."

"Very well then, you may sit."

"Thank you, sir."

I obeyed, plopping down on the chair in front of the desk. The seat springs creaked under my weight.

"At the end of this meeting, you'll go back to the barracks and forget that we ever met. Do you copy?"

"Yes, sir."

"My presence here is due to the fact that I'm going to make you a proposal that I think might interest you," the Colonel paused to open one of the desk drawers and extract another file, this one much thinner than the previous one he'd been studying when I arrived. He placed it on the dresser, just above the other one, and fixed me with his icy gaze.

"I read your service record and, quite frankly, couldn't find much in it. However, I want to make sure that the information it contains is up to date and correct. Is that all right?

"Yes, sir."

The Colonel adjusted his glasses on the bridge of his nose and opened my folder.

"It says here that your full name is Patrick Francis Coonan and that you were born on November 19, 1959, in Denver, Colorado, the son of Irish immigrants, and that today you hold the rank of sergeant in the U.S. Army Ranger Corps." A brief pause to look me in the eye again before moving forward. "It also says that you graduated with honors from Sniper School and took part in Operation Urgent Fury, during the invasion of Grenada...."

There he stopped, looked me in the eye and closed the file.

"What it doesn't say, Sergeant, is what role you played in the attack."

The Colonel remained in a frosty calm that, in a way, I found most pressing. His eyes were an impressive ice-blue color, like the very eyes of an Eskimo hound or an artic wolf. I resisted the temptation to look away, and struggled to convince myself that for nothing in the world would this man hear from my lips what I'd done in Granada.

"What, exactly, did you do there, Mr. Coonan?" He insisted.

"Excuse me, sir, but I'm not at liberty to disclose it; that information is classified. I mean, I could tell you, of course, but then I'd have to kill you."

"Now, would you really, Sergeant?"

"What, sir, tell you?"

"No; kill me," he spoke.

"Yes, I would, sir; oh, yes I would." I assured him and was forced to swallow dryly, but at least my voice didn't crack.

It was after my reply that things started to get interesting, the Colonel smiled enigmatically.

"Exactly what I expected to hear," he admitted triumphantly. "So that's what you did in Granada, wasn't it? You killed in cold blood."

For an instant, everything went swirling in my head. The past suddenly came back triggered by some images I've never been able to erase... Jungle all around me and me crawling, wearing a Ghillie suit and clutching the .50 caliber Haskins with the powerful scope... Then I heard again in my mind the roar of gunfire and the muffled silence of human targets dropping shot through the head... I blinked my eyes to force myself back to the present and confirmed that this man was looking at me intently, not missing one single detail of my reaction.

"That's what you did in Granada, didn't you?" He asked, again.

But I can be as stubborn as the next guy, and I have already said that I made a point of not admitting it.

"If it's not in my file, Colonel, it's because it never happened," and I said it firmly, to stress that the conversation was over.

He nodded, I'd say approvingly, but left his chair and walked towards me.

"Even if you don't believe it, son, I know how miserable your life is, stuck here in Fort Benning. Miss the action, huh?" At least he had the decency not to wait for an answer.

He returned to the desk and resumed his chair. Then he raised his right index finger and pointed it at me.

"I know *exactly* what you did in Granada because it was I, listen carefully, who planned your missions. There were eleven in total, Sergeant, eleven confirmed kills and all executed with a bullet through the head from a distance no less than five hundred meters."

The Colonel bit his lower lip and raised his eyebrows to emphasize his words. He put my file back in the drawer, then leaned back in his chair.

"Do you know anything about the current strategic balance in Europe?" he inquired, thus changing the subject without warning.

"No more than your average Joe, sir, but if you're referring to the mess the Soviets have made due to the deployment of our *Pershing* missiles, in Germany, I'll say yes; I read something about it in the papers."

"That's what I mean."

"I know they have responded by launching an impressive number of nuclear subs armed with ICBMs."

"That is correct; but we're both here today, not so much because of the submarines, but because of other measures that the Reds have taken. Well, one in particular: the activation of their Atomic Fang."

"I must confess I have no idea what that might be, sir."

"Very few people have. It's a state secret, you know."

"Why tell me, then?"

The Colonel sighed, but he ignored my logical question.

"After our Intelligence agencies discovered the existence of the KGB's Atomic Fang Division, no one in Washington has slept well ever since."

"Come on, sir, you're not going to tell me that the giants of the Potomac don't have a weapon capable of neutralizing this new threat..."

Once again, he ignored me, unscrupulously interrupting me in mid-sentence.

"I've been retired from the Special Forces by the DOD. I'm now in the process of recruiting the right personnel to train and lead a shadow squad of professional assassins. If you join us, Sergeant, and pass the selective training course, you'll never have to wear a uniform or carry the flag on your shoulder again. You'll wear it only in your mind and heart, and you'll work solely and exclusively under my orders."

"You're with the CIA, aren't you, sir?" I asked, but he answered immediately by shaking his head.

"Nothing further than the truth; I'm talking about eliminating the opposition at home before they get a chance to hurt us *here*. But it must be concocted with efficiency and discretion, Mr. Coonan," he finished winking at me, "do you understand?"

"Yes, sir."

"Good! I want you to think carefully about the proposal I've just made to you. We'll meet again soon, Mr. Coonan, very soon; have an answer for me then."

Chapter 5

IN ALL FAIRNESS

That evening, when New York-based P.I. Leopoldo Balmaseda entered the Manhattan salsa disco, Yuri Pavenko was sitting, as usual, at the end of the bar sipping a vodka. As soon as he arrived, the newcomer looked around, until his sharp gaze finally met the Russian's. He nodded slightly and directed his steps towards him.

"Yuri?" He asked when he reached the Russian's side. "Hi, I'm Leo."

Pavenko smiled with false kindness and said: "Hello Leo. How did you recognize me?"

The newcomer, whose imposing physique made him look like an African gorilla in a hat and trench coat, shrugged and replied: "Turk described you to me in full detail, the rest was intuition. I'm a private dick, you know," he clarified. "Of course, you're also sitting exactly where he said I'd find you; that helped."

"Ah, the old Turk! Come on, Leo, follow me; let's go find a table."

Glass in hand, the Russian left his post and led Leo to the farthest section of the room, away from the crowded dance floor. They found a vacant table and sat down. A waitress appeared as if by magic to take their order and with the same swiftness as she had materialized, she disappeared; neither man said anything until the waitress returned with the drinks. The Russian paid the tab, took out a pack of cigarettes and offered one to his guest. The waitress exchanged the littered ashtray for a clean one and left.

"Thanks for the drink and the ciggie, Yuri," Leo broke the silence. "What's on your mind?"

"Turk told me you were in the can for shooting it out with a few Brooklyn gangsters... Is this a fact?"

Leo didn't say a word, but instead he nodded with a slight shake of his head.

"Then maybe you're the man I'm looking for."

"What for?" The question was issued in a dry, direct tone.

"Protection. I need three or four bodyguards. Preferably unemployed veterans. I'm a dealer, Leo. I get shipments from overseas that can only be picked up at the dock at dawn."

Leo nodded again and took a sip of his drink.

"I mean to put you in charge of security," announced the Russian. "I have a rented apartment in Queens, where I intend to store my merchandise. If you agree to work for me, you'll do the hiring of the bodyguards, and you all will look after the shelter and my belongings. The men will fall under your command, and you'll answer directly to me. A warning," he paused to meet Leo's gaze, and for the first time since they'd met, the big man called Leo realized that this round, deceptively suave-looking stranger could be as noxious and volatile as nitroglycerin, "the competition is fierce and they might even try to push me out of the market, permanently, which is why I need keen men who can repel an armed attack. Do you understand?

Leo nodded. "Yes, absolutely. I know guys who would

even shoot it out with the Police, if necessary," he said. "Naturally, assuming that the pay motivates them."

"In that case, do you accept my conditions?"

"It all depends, Yuri. What's in it for me?"

"Twenty-five hundred a week, but I warn you that you'll remain on call twenty-four hours a day, seven days a week. Once a month, we make the short trip to the Port of Manhattan and pick up the merchandise. You and your men must be always armed, as things could go south at any given moment."

Two thousand five hundred dollars a week in those days, Leo calculated, was a lot of money.

"Okay," he said without hesitation. "When would we make the first trip?

"You'll know that as soon as you agree to work for me. So, what do you say?"

In all fairness, Leo Balmaseda said nothing; he just looked Yuri Pavenko in the eye and grinned before nodding silently.

Chapter 6

GO GET THEM, TIGER!

Several days went by before the Colonel returned to Fort Benning. When he did, I was at the outdoor range freezing my *cojones* off, perched on some rocks, watching the operations of a select group of future snipers. We all saw Commander Silas Manor drive by in his jeep, heading for the airstrip, where a civilian helicopter was currently landing. Manor stopped the jeep and waited for Col. Berkowitz to disembark. The Colonel looked like a leprechaun next to the black colossus that was our fort commander, but one mistake I've never made is to judge a man by his portliness. Napoleon and Hitler were both short in stature and everyone knows what a fight they put up. As the first time we had met, the Colonel was dressed in civilian clothes; he was wearing a narrow-brimmed hat and a gray two-piece suit under a Macintosh. He jumped out of the chopper nimbly, one hand pressing the hat against his skull and carrying an attaché case in the other. He climbed aboard the jeep and Commander Manor drove him to the barracks complex.

Once in the privacy of his office, Manor plopped down on the swivel chair behind his desk as the visitor stood in front of the window with both hands clasped behind his back. I could see them well from my position.

"How is Sgt. Coonan behaving, Commander?" the Colonel asked suddenly.

"Fine. He's been quiet since you talked to him."

"Maybe that means he's interested. I want to see him tonight, same place as before. Do you think he'll take my offer?"

"I'm sure he will, Colonel. That young man was born precisely for what you have in mind."

"Let's hope you're right, Commander. If Sgt. Coonan accepts, order his immediate transfer to Anacostia. But make it a discreet transfer, will you? You understand...."

"Yes, sir."

That same night the MP came back for me, the same oafish gorilla who carried a .45 and an M-16 assault rifle. Again, he escorted me silently down the lonely trail to the gates of The Hut, but that time, instead of being bothered by his over-blown melodrama, I felt myself smiling in the coldness of the night. These guys needed me.

Inside the shack, the Colonel was sitting at his desk with both arms folded across his chest, contemplating the thin smoke column rising from the bowl of his pipe.

"Ah, there you are, Sergeant," that was the first thing he spoke when he registered my presence, "take a seat."

"Thank you, Colonel."

"Well, I presume you've given the matter some thought, haven't you?"

"Yes, sir; I have."

"And what have you decided?"

"What do you think, Colonel? I accept."

"Splendid!" he exclaimed with unexpected enthusiasm and his ice-blue eyes sparkled. "Splendid... Welcome to the Quadrille, Mr. Coonan, that's the name of the outfit you're about to join."

The little man rose from his chair and extended his hand to me. I put mine forward and we shook them with what appeared to be — I dare say on both sides — a genuine eagerness. And with that significant gesture that sealed our destiny I could measure his strength, and I'm not only talking about his vigor, which was also obvious, but to the inexhaustible power of a steely nature, of a man who would go to the very end of the world if necessary to serve his country.... Well, it's always nice to work with people like that, isn't it?

"Do me a favor and stick around for a little while longer after I leave, Sergeant. I don't want someone to catch us leaving The Hut together. The MP will be coming for you in a little while. And, by the way, I'm Col. Marlon Berkowitz, your new commanding officer," he finally introduced himself.

Before I could say anything, Col. Berkowitz reached for his attaché case and vanished. I remained sitting down on my chair, lost in thought, feeling as pleased with myself as I have ever felt and a meek smile softening my features. The old fox had gotten to me; he *knew* I was dying to get back into action!

In the early hours of the following morning, 0300 hours to be exact, while eighty percent of the garrison was snoring in their bunks, Commander Manor himself came looking for me. His personal involvement in my transfer made me aware of the magnitude of the undertaking and, simultaneously, of how much power that parsimonious little son of a gun from Washington was capable of wielding from his clandestine do-minance. You don't wake up the commanding officer of a U.S. Army fort to have him escort a mere sergeant to the embarkation area, but — believe it or not — that's what old Silas Manor did with me. Looking back at those times reminded me that the old battle horse and I had a very special relationship, spiced by mutual respect; perhaps that was why he gave me his unconditional support from the very beginning. He was the first to realize that, when it came to sharpshooters and snipers, I was a diamond to be polished. His signed recommendation slung my promotion from volunteer recruit to the Sniper School trainee; something he did even without consulting me but convincing Pat Coonan that this was the way to go at that time was no mean feat. It seems that killing in cold blood is something I've always had in me.

Growing up in Colorado without a father — my old man, a Denver cop, was killed in the line of duty when I was two years old — was perhaps the most powerful reason that impelled me to embark on a military career; you know, the classic "follow in your father's footsteps" and all that, but that certainly wasn't the only motive... I talked about that at the beginning of my story, it was the cold rejection to become my wife I got from that beautiful Irish girl in my neighborhood who used to call herself my girlfriend: the Kellys' daughter.

I kept reflecting on my past during the ride to the runway in Commander Manor's jeep. I was no longer dressed in uniform, but in a long-sleeved, heather-gray sweatshirt under a plaid wool jacket and faded Levi's. The waiting eggbeater was already warming up its engines and Manor stopped the jeep, gave me a friendly pat on the shoulder and grinned.

"Go get them, Tiger; our nation claims you," he hissed. "Hit them hard where it counts and make me proud!"

It was a wolfish grin that twisted his mouth under the bushy mustache before he finished off with an effusive:

"Kick some ass!!"

When I said good-bye to him, I was also smiling bursting of that blind self-sufficiency that generates an excellent physical condition and the divine youth, nodding my head emphatically before reaching for my backpack to jump out of the jeep. I felt like a restless hunting mastiff who had been ordered to go after the prey.

Minutes later, I was aboard the chopper flying towards Anacostia Naval Base.

*C*hapter 7

PREPARATIONS

The following day at noon, in the borough of Queens, New York City, a taxi from Yellow Cab braked in front of Yuri Pavenko's apartment building. The rear doors of the vehicle opened, and Leo Balmaseda followed the Russian saboteur out of the cab. The latter paid the driver and dismissed him. Left alone on the street, employer and employee looked at each other and the KGB man motioned for Leo to follow him inside. Once in the apartment, Balmaseda could see that it was a spartan place, furnished with everyday items: a gas heater, a medium-sized TV set and a worn leather couch. In the kitchen there was a dining room set with a table and four chairs. The master bedroom had a king-sized bed; the second bedroom a medium-sized one.

Returning to the living room, after showing him around, Pavenko rubbed both his hands and inquired:

"Well, what do you think?"

Leo shrugged his shoulders.

"Not bad. The merchandise can be kept in the master bedroom, protected by one of my men. The other two can sleep in the second bedroom. I will take the couch to keep the door always guarded," he paused. "Let me warn you that I won't be able to stay in this place twenty-four hours a day. As I said before, I have a private investigations firm to attend to."

"That won't be a problem, as long as the apartment is guarded around the clock," said the Russian. "If you must move, get people who can stay here overnight and rotate them. That's your problem, Leo. But let me warn you that I will hold *you* responsible if this shelter is raided and there is no one here to defend it. Are we clear?"

Again, the Russian's fake cordiality vanished, and Big Leo didn't like the menacing suspense that followed. Nonetheless, he nodded with forced meekness and walked to the door, where he busied himself examining the lock.

"This needs to be changed," he said, "I also need a floorplan of the building with all available evacuation routes in case of a contingency."

Pavenko grinned. "I'm very pleased to hear you say that. Could you get the blueprints?"

"Yes, but I will need some dough; I can also buy new locks and get you a more effective alarm system...."

"Money is not an impediment. Tell me how much and when."

"Relax, Yuri. First, I need to make some calculations."

"All right, Leo, that's fine with me."

After that they didn't see each other again for a few days. Yuri left confident that the man he had hired for the job was a capable guy. And of course, he was.

However, the Russian saboteur had no idea who he was really dealing with.

*C*hapter *8*

THE RECRUITING

Once he had seen — and thoroughly reviewed — the apartment where Yuri Pavenko intended to set up his clandestine safehouse, Leo Balmaseda focused on the next task on the agenda: recruiting the gunmen who would integrate the team in charge of security. After some thought, he opted for only three, instead of four. Five men, including himself, would feel a bit un-comfortable there and his experience in such matters, which was vast, advised him to minimize any point of conflict between people of volatile character. That's what decided him.

The first one that came to his mind was Mack Dempsey, a mercenary who was known as Candy Mack throughout Hell's Kitchen, because of his deceptively boyish face, with a Robert Redford-like square jaw and cute dimples under his cheeks when he smiled. Mack was freckled, had reddish hair and eyes too blue to be true. In the unlikely event that his ruddy appearance did not betray his Irish blood, the locality in which he moved around certainly did. In addition to being a Vietnam vet, Candy Mack was well connected in the New York underworld and could always be reached at McCoy's, one of the oldest establishments located in the heart of

Hell's Kitchen, a distinctly Irish neighborhood if you must know, of dubious reputation, near the Midtown Business District.

Leo was aware that the pub was open seven days a week, with happy hour runs lasting from 10 A.M. to 7 P.M. and its nightly equivalent from 11 P.M. till 4 A.M. of the following day. But the nightly rounds did not extend for all seven days, only on Thursdays and Sundays; on Friday and Saturday nights, the pub remained closed. So, he chose a Wednesday to show up around midnight — a habit that, I supposed, had rubbed off on him from hanging out with Yuri.

He first took a cab in Jackson Heights and told the cabby to drive aimlessly through the streets parallel to the Hudson River, so he could spot if anyone was following him. When he was satisfied he had no tail, the New York Rican shamus gave the driver the address of his destination: 768 9th Avenue, between 51st and 52nd Street. On the way, they passed 47th and 48th, where the Time Warner Center stands, and once again he checked that no one was following him. Leo was armed, of course, he packed a Smith & Wesson .38 Special revolver, with five rounds in the cylinder: all of them hollow-points. He could afford this luxury because, being a professional private eye, he was licensed to carry arms by the State of New York.

Finally, the taxi stopped in front of the pub. Leo paid the stipulated fee to the cab driver, abandoned the vehicle, and crossed the street on foot. He didn't find Mack drinking at the bar; the red-haired merc was sitting quietly in a booth for two, savoring a pint of lager with a certain reluctance. The beer had been poured in a conical, thick glass tumbler, which bore the name McCoy's embossed in gold letters. Leo checked that Candy Mack was alone before approaching him.

Flashing a baleful smile, the investigator took a seat across from red-haired Dempsey without a word.

"What are you drinking?" asked Mack as he recognized the newcomer and motioned the bartender over.

"Whatever you are."

"Two pints of lager, Willie," Candy ordered the bartender, before turning to Leo. "What brings you to these parts of the jungle, partner? You're out of your territory."

"Are you involved in something at present, or can you be hired? I've got a little job waiting for you; I mean if you're interested. A grand a week."

"One thousand dollars *per week* you say, you bastard... But of course!"

"I need a couple of guys like you as soon as possible, can you recommend someone?

Mack showed him one of his falsely candid smiles before admitting: "Hell, bro, I sure can!"

Finding the other gunmen was as easy for Mack Dempsey as it was for Leo to locate him. Dempsey had already worked with the other candidates on several occasions, and they seemed to mesh well. The better of the two was a small black guy named Lucas Jackson, nicknamed Black Lucas by some, whom Mack respected greatly because he'd served with him in Nam and had quite a reputation as a disciplined professional soldier of fortune. Some rumors associated his past with the Black Panther Party during the late 1960s. I understand that the BPP was formed in '66, when two black militants, Huey Percy Newton, and Bobby Seale, began to think that Dr. Martin Luther King's peaceful campaign had failed to achieve its goal and it was necessary

53

to resort to violence.

When Candy Mack made the telephone call that would put him in contact with Black Lucas, the latter was busy satisfying one of his many mistresses. Still entangled with that beautiful mulatto girl from the Bronx who seemed to want to squeeze him like an orange between her legs, Jackson got rid of her as best he could and went to answer the call on the second phone line of his Harlem apartment, the one that when it rang could only mean a possibility of employment.

The third man was not as competent, but Candy Mack had taken pity on him at some point in his life and, besides, he owed the dude past favors; so, he brought him into the deal as well. That turned out to be a mistake. You are, or become, only as good, or bad, as the people you surround yourself with. It's something that I first learned from Commander Manor, a concept that Col. Berkowitz also instilled in me.

Chapter 9

DESTINATION: ANACOSTIA

My arrival at the huge naval installation named Anacostia proved to be unique for me in more ways than I'd imagined. An officious guide who came to greet me gave me a tour of the base, not bothering to reveal his real name and — just as the Colonel had done in our first interview at Ft. Benning — instructing me to call him "sir," or "master." *Very typical of all these cloak-and-dagger frat boys*, I thought, but I opted to keep my mouth shut and not say anything that might come back to haunt me in the long run. So, I obliged.

He was a tall, muscular gent, who looked very much like the actor James Caan, Sonny Corleone in the *The Godfather* movie, with trapeze artist shoulders and a flattened nose as the epicenter of a harsh, gaunt, square-chinned face. He could have been in his late thirties or early forties. He also, like Marlon Berkowitz, had the glaucous eyes of an Eskimo hound, or an Arctic wolf. One detail that struck me about the fellow was his pallor; I reflected that if he were not ill it was probably due to a prolonged stay in the Nordic regions of the planet; perhaps in Eastern Europe, behind the Iron Curtain... If he were American or held any rank in the U.S. Army, he did not outwardly state it. Eventually I came to learn who he was, of course, but that did not happen until near the end of my training; at the time of my arrival at Anacostia, the identity of this "master" was unknown to me.

After giving me the orientation tour of the base, he led me to the building where I would receive my specialized training and showed me to my room. When I asked how many more recruits would be sharing the class with me, he replied that this information was not yet available and that we would not begin group training for at least a couple of weeks. Not all the participants had arrived yet. He added that I shouldn't worry about anything, as my pay grade had been increased considerably by leaving Fort Benning and I was already upgraded to danger pay even if not much was demanded of me during those two weeks.

Fine by me, I thought. I could use a little break.

The next thing he did was hand me a slim file, the contents of which consisted of eight neatly typed pages. It turned out to be a manual explaining different ways of how to carry out a cold-blooded murder.

"Take this as a prelude to your training but take it seriously. Almost everything you're going to find in there has been prepared by a scientific mind for the CIA. It's all hypothetical but memorize it anyway. Trust me, the information will come handy when it's your turn to go out in the field."

My initial reaction was to give this assassin's manual a cynical and contemptuous glance, but once again my military training clicked in, and I managed to control my strong desire to throw the booklet on the floor and stomp on it. *Who the fuck does this guy think he is?* I thought. *To come and teach me how to kill in cold blood? Me? A veteran Ranger sniper?*

"Yes, sir," was my grim reply.

As if he'd guessed what gnawed at me inside, the "master" smiled mischievously and said: "Look, Coonan, I know very well that you are the impatient type and that, like most recruits coming into this unit, you come here looking to get in right on the action. There's no need to rush, believe me when I tell you that we have enough work to keep all of you very busy. Well, I mean those who pass the selection course."

"Study that manual, soldier, read it thoroughly, and memorize it from cover to cover; I'll be waiting for you tomorrow in the cafeteria at 0800 hours for breakfast together. There I will hand you more interesting material to memorize. Understood?"

"Yes, sir."

I withdrew to my room with the intention of reading those eight pages, but I did no more than lie down and put my head on the pillow and I fell asleep. All that rattling and the excitement of starting a new life away from the barracks as an undercover operative had caused me some mental exhaustion. After a couple of hours, I woke up, took a shower, and put on a set of pajamas before returning to bed and giving myself over to reading....

"This text will be used as part of the introduction to define what is the premeditated slaughter of any target outside of the killer's jurisdiction. A person sentenced to die by an organization, whose physical elimination will bring advantages to that entity...."

Since what I was really interested in were the procedures and rules of engagement described in the manual, I opted to skip the introduction, which was nothing more than a study of the origins of the word assassin, going back to the distant times of Hasan al Sabbah.

"No order for assassination shall be written on paper

or transmitted on a phonetic recording. The order will be given directly to the executor by a single person. The fewer people involved in the project, the better.

"It is possible to kill in cold blood using only the hands, but few people possess the necessary skill to do it properly. However, an axe, a hammer, a wrench, a screwdriver, a kitchen knife, the metal base of a lamp, the use of any of these instruments can work...."

I made a mental note to find a way to immunize myself against the Cowboy syndrome, if I intended to become an eliminator for the Quadrille, but deep down I had my doubts on the assumption that I'm a born hunter, firearms and their accessories have always played a preponderant role in my life.

"A leather belt, a piece of rope, cable or wire will also do if the killer is agile and strong enough. All these improvised weapons, when in hand, offer the advantage of not causing suspicion....

"In a situation where the assassin is searched for a concealed weapon, before carrying out his mission or after he has completed it, it is imperative that no conventional weapon of any kind be found hidden in his clothing....

"Staged accidents are the best technique that can be employed, if carefully planned and executed. The most efficient of all methods is to cause a fall on a hard surface from a height of twenty meters. Examples: pushing the victim down an elevator shaft, down a staircase, from a high window and from a bridge. The best way to do this is to hold the target firmly by the ankles and throw them over the railing. In the statistics, falls are the least investigated causes of death by authorities....

"Another frequently used method is to push the target so that he or she falls into the sea or a river, but

this only works if the person cannot swim. The victim's panic can be used against him, if the killer also jumps into the water pretending to come to his aid while finishing the job....

"If the situation allows it, it is good to study the habits of the mark before planning the attack. Example: A mark given to ingesting large portions of alcohol is vulnerable to dying from excess alcohol....

"Pushing someone in front of a train at a railway station, or in a subway in the city always carries risks. It also requires great skill and good timing and may attract the attention of witnesses....

"Whenever possible, faked car accidents should be avoided because they attract attention. But if the killer chooses to do so, then the best tactic is to get the victim drunk or drugged and sit him/her behind the wheel. This technique has its risks and only works well if the vehicle can be pushed down a slope or cliff into deep water if there are no witnesses....

"Fires can also be profitable if the target is drugged and burned in an abandoned building. Narcotics are often very effective when applied to this kind of murder. An overdose of morphine, for example, is painless, lethal, and almost impossible to detect. But if the victim turns out to be a drug addict, then the overdose must be increased, although in the most common cases 130 grams is what is used. If the mark turns out to be a heavy drinker, as soon as he/she loses consciousness the killer will proceed to inject him with morphine, or a similar substance, and hope that the cause of death will be labeled as acute ethyl intoxication...."

At that point I paused for a few minutes to take a breather, use the toilet, and make myself a cup of coffee. All that information was new to me, it belonged to a different level of assassination than the one employed by the pros in the world I had dwelled in until then.

Everything I had read began to raise a world of concerns for me; was this really the path I wanted to follow? What did I want to do with my life? When the Colonel recruited me in The Hut, I harbored the romantic notion that my duty would be to fight the deadly Communist agents operating in our streets, using silenced pistols, the strength of my muscles and the wiles I had learned on the battlefield. But now, reading the CIA's *Assassins training manual* was like being slapped in the face. But again, I summoned my self-control and iron military discipline not to reveal my true feelings, much less to this "master" who served as my guide, whenever I saw the man again. I said to myself, if this was the only way things were done in the Quadrille, then the job was not for me, but that was something I would only discuss with Col. Berkowitz personally — if it came to that.

Then another consideration came to mind, and it made me wonder if this might not be the strategy the old fox employed to separate the men from the boys, giving the new recruits a more depressing — or macabre, if you will — version that projects that warring ardor and patriotic heroism many of us cultivate in the military. The war that Marlon Berkowitz was going to fight with the Quadrille was a low and dirty war, in the most pestilent sewers and dark alleys of our cities, where it would be necessary to get down and dirty, battling a sordid foe that did not attack head-on but with portable nuclear bombs, which would detonate underhandedly in overpopulated areas not only by men, but also by women, elders and children miles away from the front lines.

I had to cling to that thought to force myself to read

on; I'd been recruited not to win medals or reap public glory; we were only asked to exterminate the vermin that gnawed at our insides.

And it was by coercing myself to think like this that I resumed my reading.

"All blows should be aimed at that part of the head behind the ears and at the base of the skull. The lower and frontal part of the face, comprised from the eyebrows to the neck, can withstand more punishment without suffering mortal consequences....

"In the execution of an attack, the use of firearms (it has been proven) does not work as well as the previously mentioned techniques. A common problem is the assassin's lack of knowledge of the limitations of the weapon of choice. Most shooters expect much better performance than guns offer....

"Refrain from using hand grenades, or any other type of homemade bombs that can be tossed at the target. The use of explosives should be avoided at all costs, but if one is forced to use fragmentary material, they should use a minimum quantity of four and a half kilograms. The fragments may be of stone or metal and should be the shape and size of a walnut, not a pencil. It is preferable to use explosive substances that are of military ordinance or intended for commercial use, rather than homemade explosives. Anti-personnel mines are the most effective weapons, provided the assassin has been well trained in their use. The target must be not less than six feet away from the explosive charge at the time of detonation...."

I closed the file and stared at the ceiling without seeing it for some time, reflecting. I can only tell you that that first night in Anacostia it was not possible for me to sleep well.

The next morning, I could not find my "master" in the

cafeteria: the man simply did not show up. It didn't take long for me to realize that something anomalous was going down at the base; some of those around me in the mess hall sat in doomsday silence and in their hollow eyes there were traces of underhanded apprehension, although none deigned to share with me what was causing such a tense situation. But everyone on the base staff seemed to be expecting the most terrible news. The other "master" I was sent to replace the absent one confirmed this.

He came over to where I'd been sitting with two identical trays carrying our breakfasts and he was kind enough to place one on the table in front of me. I couldn't help but notice that under his right armpit he carried a file very similar to the one I had been lent the day before, although this one was much thicker.

Well, my original "guide" had mentioned that there would be more interesting material, hadn't he? This was it.

"Your instructor will not be available today, Mr. Coonan," said the new guide as he prepared to sink his teeth into the food. "He sent me as a substitute. Here is your breakfast."

I thanked him and took an anxious look at the food; the aroma it exuded was exquisite. A creamy omelet with ham and melted Cheddar cheese crowned the plate, accompanied by a couple of English muffins with real butter and strawberry jam, a portion of freshly baked cakes and the steaming cup of coffee, which I would have killed for in a heartbeat, had the occasion arisen.

"Thank you, sir, you're really very kind," I murmured before I started churning through the edibles.

"No problem, would you like some orange juice? I can pour you a glass."

"Yes, please; I'd appreciate it."

"All right; I'll be right back."

The mystery behind the strange situation in the base had not dampened my appetite, but I still refrained from touching my plate until the substitute returned with my juice and took a seat. When he reached for his fork and knife, I jumped my food.

"Did you get a chance to read the file last night?" he asked softly without looking up from his plate.

"I did, sir; I read every word of the article and more than once."

"Good; what did you think of the text?"

"I found it very interesting, sir, witty too; certainly, practical in every way."

He smiled. "But it's not your thing, is it?"

I grinned, though I was careful not to utter comments that would inconvenience him.

"I'm here to serve the country and do what I'm ordered, sir. Nothing else."

"Pleased to hear your answer, Mr. Coonan," he said before pointing his index finger toward the thick file he had brought with him, and which now rested next to him on the table. "This new reading material I bring you differs slightly in content from the first folder. The information you will find between its covers is going to draw you a profile of the adversary you are about to face."

"You're referring to the KGB, right?"

"Yes, the KGB and at least one other foreign Intelligence service that operates in conjunction with the Soviets, here, in the American continent."

"I see."

"As you can appreciate, this dossier is thicker. There is much more material to assimilate in it; therefore, I suggest that you return to your quarters as soon as you have finished your breakfast and apply yourself to study.

I will join you here at 1300 hours. You copy?"

"Yes, sir."

The report was superb and provided me with an extensive and detailed view of the organization and its purposes, but what really caught my eye was the section entitled WEAPONS. All enemy agents were trained in the use of the AK-47 light assault rifle, with folding stock and banana clip; the 9-millimeter Makarov pistol and the so-called PSM, which fires a 5.45 x 18-millimeter cartridge and was their weapon of choice for operating covertly, as it is easier to conceal under clothing.

There were other weapons in their arsenal that deserved my attention as well because they were unconventional and camouflaged; some even looked like circus tricks, like the ingenious flask that fired poisoned pellets. The Bulgarians added to the arsenal the key ring-pistols, which fired .32 caliber bullets and did not detonate the alarms of the detectors at the airfields. Sets of mini daggers concealed in shoe heels. Special coins reinforced with a saw blade. An umbrella with a poisonous tip. And the typical lip crayon for women that fired a single 4.5-millimeter slug and can be hidden in any body orifice to pass undetected by security checkpoints.

The section entitled MODUS OPERANDI also caught my attention. Contrary to our CIA, which during the tenure of the late Allen Dulles had indulged in electronic espionage called SIGNINT — consisting of surveillance of the satellites we have in orbit, calculations, and computerized photos — the KGB preferred to rely on the HUMINT — or human intelligence — method and concentrated its efforts on recruiting double-agents, using its charming Marxist ideology as a hook. But after the Hungarian massacre, in the 1956 uprising, the *Komitet's* tactics had changed and they were now resorting, more and more frequently and with better results, to the things that never fail: bribery and blackmail.

As I said, it was an excellent report and I read it not once, not twice, but three times, until every detail was etched into my memory, eager as I was to immerse myself in all these issues. In the section attached to the KGB file, the Cuban General Directorate of Intelligence was mentioned. There they explained that after Castro took power by force of arms, exactly in 1963, shortly after the October Crisis, the Soviets invited a total of fifteen hundred DGI agents to participate in a training program that was conducted in Moscow. Seven years later, a team of KGB advisors flew to Cuba to oversee a purge of DGI personnel that eliminated all Cuban agents suspected of being anti-Soviet. Why? Some will ask, and I will answer them by quoting an article from *The New York Times* that defined the Cuban Intelligence service as "a capable spy engine that achieves results." The *Times* write-up described it as one of the most extensive and effective security services in the world, despite the island's tiny size and meager domestic economy.

This is how I learned that the DGI was made up of six divisions divided into two categories: *Operations & Support*. Operations comprised political and economic intelligence, further subdivided into four sections labeled: *Eastern Europe, North America*; *Western Europe*; *Africa/Asia/Latin America*. This last category also included Foreign Counterintelligence and Military Intelligence in its functions. On the other hand, the support divisions included technical support — communications, false documentation, and encrypted messages — and information and combat preparation (intelligence analysis).

When it became time to meet my new guide at lunchtime, the substitute did not appear. This time it was my original "master" who showed up at the cafeteria for the occasion. It was also he who brought me the lunch tray, as the substitute had done at breakfast time, and he took a seat opposite me with an identical platter. This repeated treatment, to which I was not accustomed — let's clarify that at Fort Benning no one ever brought me lunch or breakfast — seemed to me to be a psychological strategy used by the cloak-and-dagger boys, to create links between students and teachers; at least, for as long as the course lasted.

Lunch consisted of meatloaf with gravy, mashed potatoes, creamed spinach with melted Cheddar on top, and roasted corn on the cob. It tasted great!

"I apologize for leaving you briefly, Mr. Coonan. Something came up that has placed us all on high alert."

His face wore a grim expression as he spoke, so I presumed he was serious.

"Yuri Andropov, First Secretary of the Communist Party of the USSR, died yesterday."

"What?!" I burst out, and almost choked on the news. "Are you kidding me?"

My spontaneous reaction was never due to doubting his word, I must explain, but to the fact that only fifteen months earlier, the same had happened with Chairman Leonid Brezhnev, whom Andropov had replaced.

"He was not as old as he looked, but it seems that he suffered from kidney problems."

"Did we know this was going to happen?" I asked.

"There were certain indications, yes, that the man had become ill and that he had been absent from his post for almost six months..." He paused significantly to look me in the eye. "Don't get your hopes up, soldier; his death won't change things. Someone else will sit in his chair and the party will continue; that's all. They're going to keep on trying to screw up our lives and we are going to stop them dead. Is that clear?"

"Yes, sir!"

There was an ominous silence that reigned between us for a few seconds, until I asked him: "Do we know who the successor is?"

"Not yet, but I'm sure someone in our State Department will have a good idea by now," he said, and his thin, cruel-looking lips parted into a grim smile. "Like I said, Mr. Coonan, nothing is going to change. The Cold War continues, son. You'll see."

And boy was he right!

On the eleventh day of February 1984, *The New York Times* published the following article signed by journalist John F. Burns:

YURI ANDROPOV HAS DIED IN MOSCOW; REAGAN APPOINTS VICE PRESIDENT BUSH TO ATTEND THE FUNERAL

(As Soviet leader, Yuri V. Andropov faced major problems with the West and an impoverished domestic economy. His obituary appears on page 9.)

MOSCOW, Feb. 10 – *The Soviet leadership announced today that Yuri V. Andropov ceased to exist on Thursday, just over a year after he replaced Leonid I. Brezhnev as general secretary of the Communist Party of the USSR; he was 69 years old. The two-paragraph announcement was read in the media at 2:30 P.M. (6:30 A.M. New York time) and was repeated throughout the day, followed by a series of bulletins regarding the cause of his death and arrangements for his funeral next*

Tuesday.

Konstantin U. Chernenko, 72, a Brezhnev protégé who served as secretary, will preside over the funeral. Foreign diplomats have interpreted this news as an indication that it will be Chernenko who will replace Andropov in his position...

The new Soviet leader, as it would be announced later to the entire world, was now Konstantin Chernenko, another one of the hard-liners protected by Brezhnev for almost thirty years.

In any case, my master-instructor was right: *Nothing* had changed!

*C*hapter *10*

HESITATIONS

Four months later, at the KGB headquarters in Central Moscow, Andrei Kodina, chief of staff of the Atomic Fang Division, sat again in Maj. Anatoly Kirov's office, taking small sips from a steaming cup of tea. Kodina, the man dressed in civilian clothes, seemed worried, while the major looked at him in hermetic silence with malevolent eyes. After a few seconds, Maj. Kirov decided to break his ominous muteness.

"How is the plan coming along?" He inquired.

"Smooth, comrade Major. I have received acknowledgment of receipt for the first four shipments to New York. The agent in charge of the operation is following his orders to the letter."

Kirov drank more tea and said: "Well, Yuri has an extraordinary record. However, there is something that has started to bother me."

"Something?" Kodina asked, beginning to worry. "What do you mean?"

"Will he have the courage to do it? Will Yuri detonate the bomb when ordered?"

Kodina answered nervously. "But of course, comrade! Yuri is a very resourceful and experienced agent. Furthermore, he was approved by me for the mission."

Following his response, Kirov leaned in his seat.

"That is *precisely* where I want to go, comrade chief of staff. It was *you* who supervised his training; it was *you* who recommended him; *you* approved his involvement in this operation..." an ominous pause. "Who do *you* think will fall to blame if Yuri isn't able to perform as expected at the pivotal moment?"

The chief of staff looked away from the major's hardened face and swallowed dryly.

"Well, I think comrade Pavenko can pull this off," he replied. "He is the best operative in the entire Atomic Fang Division."

"Maybe he is, I don't dispute it, but there's something about this individual that has begun to worry me..."

"Do you think I overlooked something important, comrade Major?" Kodina barged in.

"I don't know... I can't point out any specific details, but there is *something* that doesn't quite add up here; I sense it. You see, making Manhattan disappear from the face of the Earth with a 10-kiloton atomic bomb is no ordinary task, comrade, and Agent Yuri has lived in that extraordinary city for more than a decade." The major paused to stare at him coldly. "Furthermore, his record indicates that he is a hedonist and perfectly fits into the rotten environment that prevails in that capitalist Gomorrah. Yuri goes all out for expensive call girls, Western fashions, high-tech appliances, and the nightlife of exotic cabarets and extravagant discos, the luxury hotels, etcetera... Who knows how many other vices the man has acquired?!"

"Perhaps there is a way we can control him," Kodina said in a soft tone.

"Seriously? From here? How the hell are you planning to achieve that?" Kirov hissed. "If you have an idea, comrade, share it! I'm all ears!"

"We have a contact in Manhattan: a woman. She is Cuban by birth, and used to be an agent of the Cuban DGI before we made her our operative. In fact, it was she whom we employed to activate the mission."

"Mirta? The Velasco woman?"

"Yes! We could use her as a guarantee. She is resourceful girl and can always keep Yuri under surveillance without the man becoming suspicious. I know that comrade Pavenko has a special weakness for her, Major. Yuri is an admirer of Latin culture..."

"I know, I know," Kirov intruded fastidiously, "it's in his file; the comrade enjoys Latin music," then he smiled grimly, "he also loves the Latin culture *and* Latin women. Why do you mention it, comrade? Has he tried to seduce her?"

Kodina smiled. "Several times, Major," he rushed to answer, "I have read the reports she sends us."

"And this woman... does she correspond to him?"

The chief of staff expanded his smile in an enigmatic way: "Not exactly in the way you imply, but Mirta is capable of going to bed with anyone if it's demanded of her during the course of an operation."

"I see" Kirov crossed his arms and frowned, before muttering: "Mm."

*C*hapter *11*

COMPLICATIONS

Meanwhile, at Pavenko's apartment building in the borough of Queens, Leo Balmaseda had worked hard to convert the flat into a real safehouse. Security had been tightened to its maximum with a new alarm system and better door locks. The Russian agent was pleased with the outcome. The conversion was done with the assistance of Mack Dempsey, Lucas Jackson, and the one they called Hippy Rick — we learned later that this man's real name was Richard Byers. Mr. Byers was the third member of the unemployed vets Pavenko had suggested for hiring in his first interview with the New York P.I.

The night Leo chose to perform an unexpected security check, Black Lucas was lying down on the couch smoking a joint and watching a football game on the TV; he was dressed in faded jeans and a long-sleeved gray sweatshirt. Over the sweatshirt he wore the harness of a shoulder holster, where he carried a 9mm Browning Hi-power semiauto. Mack Dempsey was sitting in the dining room next to the kitchen, playing cards with his buddy Rick, whose shabby looks resembled those of a homeless man or — surprise, surprise — a filthy hippy. Both men were strapped with shoulder holsters like the one worn by the black mercenary.

Being the colossus he was, Mack packed a powerful .357 Magnum fitted with an 8-inch barrel and fixed sights. Rick favored a Taurus .32 ACP semiauto. A shitty little handgun, if you ask me — I'd rather work with American-made firearms — but then Hippy Rick was sort of a shitty creature....

"Hey, guys!" cried out Lucas from the living room. "It's been a while since I played, and I'm sick of watching this crappy game. C'mon, Rick, bring your skinny ass over here and park it in the couch. Watch some football, dude!"

Rick turned his cards on the table with a triumphant smile. "Your ass is mine, Mack. Again."

"Fuck!" Mack blurted out.

"I'm going for a break, buddy. Need to take a leak." He turned toward the living room and raised his voice. "All yours, Luc. I'm out of the game."

That's when the front door opened with a bang and Leo stepped into the apartment holding a short-barrel Smith & Wesson revolver.

"Bang! Bang! Bang!" He shouted, "You are all dead!"

Upon hearing the "shots" Black Lucas and Candy Mack, taken by surprise, dived for cover and began to roll on the floor in opposite directions, both desperately struggling to draw their holstered weapons. Rick didn't even move, he just stood there watching Leo with a scornful smile on his face; then he stretched his body and yawned loudly without a care in the world.

His two companions got up, but since they were ashamed for being caught with their pants down — axiomatically speaking — both kept their heads down, to avoid their boss's furious gaze.

"You fuckin' idiots!!!" Leo cried out after closing the door and bolting it. "When will you learn to keep the door always locked, huh?!"

"I'm sorry, Leo," mumbled Mack, "it was my fault, you left me in charge and I... uh... I promise you it won't happen again."

"Of course you are responsible, you big white ape!!" the New York Rican shouted. He quickly walked up to Mac and pushed up the barrel of his Smith & Wesson under Dempsey's chin: "The next time you fail me, you are dead, you hear. You are fuckin' dead!!!"

Then Leo brushed Mack aside, turned around and quickly walked up to Lucas, though this time he left the gun pointing at the floor.

He got in front of the little black man and looked down at him, breathing hard. "And *that* goes for you too, you damn fool...."

Lucas also backed down; through the marijuana-induced haze that clouded his brain, he knew, as well as his buddy Mack, that they were at fault. You don't get paid a grand per week to let the boss walk in on you and catch you with your guard down. No, sir!

"Rule number one," spat Leo, "keep the door *always* latched. Rule number two: If two of you are playing cards in the dining room area, the third man *must* keep his eyes on the door, get it? You had *your* back to the door, Lucas, while your two mates here played cards!!" He shouted, pointing a thick index finger at the black mercenary.

"I'm sorry, boss. I, uh... I really am." Jackson mumbled humbly. "It won't happen again."

Leo turned around to face Rick, expecting the same reaction he'd gotten from his teammates, but the hippy didn't look affected at all. In fact, he was grinning placidly, as if the situation in which they found themselves was something funny. Rick's demeanor was incredibly serene, or *cool* — as they said in those days.

"Shit, and I thought you guys were pros!!" snorted Leo as he walked now toward Byers. "But *you*, flea-market hippy, *you* are the worst!" The big New York Rican was furious, he leaped towards Rick with unsuspected swiftness in a man his size and grabbed the grinning hippy by his oversized shirt lapels, bringing his rage-contorted mug close to the skinny Byers's face.

"Have you been drinking, Leo?" Hippy Rick giggled, struggling to move away. "Man, your breath stinks, god damnit, get off my face!"

Leo didn't waste time with more verbal insults, he just punched Rick hard on the nose. Blood splattered, Byers took three steps back and landed on his rear end on the dining room floor.

He touched his nose and for a couple of seconds he stared at the blood in disbelief. "You broke my nose, you goddamned greaser!" He shouted at the top of his lungs. "Oh, man, I'm going to kill you for this!"

Leo allowed him to get back on his feet and threw another punch at him. However, this time Rick ducked in time to avoid getting hit on the nose again and threw himself at the New York Rican. Both men collided and went down hard in a tangle of punching arms and kicking legs. On the floor, Leo rolled over and came up on top of Rick, managing to pin him down with his formidable weight. Leo straddled Byers and im-mobilized the other man's arms with his knees. Rick grunted and desperately struggled to free his upper extremities, but soon realized his efforts were futile.

Lucas tried to stop the scuffle before it got worse, but Candy Mack, who knew Leo well and feared that Luke's gesture would be mistaken for aggression, held him back and signaled him not to get involved.

On the floor, Leo grabbed a handful of Hippy Rick's long, greasy hair and pulled down hard to the left, forcing him to tilt his head and strain his neck, exposing it. Then he took out a pocketknife, released the blade with a well-rehearsed flick of the wrist and pressed its sharp point against the other man's Adam's apple.

"What did you say you were going to do?" hissed Leo.

Still showing defiance, though unable to free himself, Rick spat on Leo's face. Leo responded by sinking the tip of the blade an eighth of an inch into Hippy Rick's Adam's apple, drawing blood.

"What did you say you were going to do, huh?" Repeated Leo.

"Get your fat ass off me, you Bronx scum! I'm going to kill...!!"

Rick stopped mid-sentence, unable to finish what he'd started to say. No one could without a voice — or a throat, for that matter. Leo sliced it open with his blade and rolled off him quickly to avoid being touched by the geyser of blood that erupted from the wound.

For a few seconds an unearthly silence dangled over the dining room, only broken by the quiet gurgle of Rick's blood and the gases emanating from his opened Adam's apple. Leo wiped the blood off his blade on the dead man's shirt and stood up with the pocketknife gripped in his right hand. There was still a lot of violence left in him when he turned to face both Black Lucas and Candy Max.

"You need to get this piece of shit out of here," he spoke softly to them as if nothing had happened, "throw the corpse in the bathtub, for now. I'll see what to do with it later," then he yelled, "C'mon you two, get cracking!!"

Both mercs rushed to do what they'd been ordered, neither of them felt like contradicting Leo after what had taken place. Can't say I blame them, though; Leo was a tough customer, sure, as tough as they come, but he was also the goose of the golden eggs, their ticket to a thousand bucks per week for as long as this assignment lasted....

When they returned from the bathroom, Leo walked to the door, opened it halfway and turned around to face them before leaving the apartment.

"I have to step out now, but I will be back with a car to get the corpse out of here," he finished pocketing the knife, now that it was obvious that he wasn't going to have any trouble with the rest of the crew, "and lock the bloody door behind me, will you? *Stay alert!*"

As soon as Leo abandoned the Queen's safehouse, he walked a few blocks east and got into a vacant public phone booth. He had checked for unwanted tails, but no one was following him. Inside the booth he picked up the receiver, put in a nickel and a dime first, then punched in the contact number Yuri had given him for emergencies and waited for an answer. He got a recording machine at the other end of the line and left a message for the Russian agent to meet him in one hour at the Manhattan salsa disco. The rule among them was always to give the other party (at least) an hour before a meeting upon request.

Leo was about to kill two birds with one stone; first he was going to brief Pavenko on Rick's death, and then ask him for a new means of transport. The car he'd been given for the trips to the South Street Seaport Mall had broken down that very same morning, and they needed a replacement ASAP.

He had no idea at the time that things would turn out at the disco the way they did.

Pavenko was punctual, as usual; when he arrived, the Russian found the big New York Rican waiting for him sitting, as was their custom, by the end of the bar counter. There was a vacant stool next to Leo's, so Yuri took it.

"What the hell is wrong? When I hired you, you assured me you could handle any trouble by yourself."

Leo was taken aback by the hostile tone in his boss's harsh voice. He shifted his weight on the stool and put a hand on Yuri's shoulder to calm down the Russian.

"Easy, boss, there's no problem. Not anymore, I took care of it. Just wanted to report."

"Okay, what is it?"

"One of the men... Look, today I decided to run a security check on the safehouse. I showed up without warning and surprised them. Two of them reacted the way they should have — well, more, or less — but the third one failed the test."

"And?"

"Well, I came down hard on them and put them in their places, but the one who failed the test took the chewing personally and disrespected me in front of the others... I killed the fuck, that's all." He paused for a second before continuing: "Aside from that minor inconvenience, the car broke down. We need another one."

Pavenko was shocked at Leo's off-handed way of confessing to a murder, he had already heard Turk saying that the big New York Rican P.I. was as tough as they come, but, inside Yuri's well-trained brain, a red flag was raised. That kind of psychological callousness — when it came to killing human beings — was only achieved by trained pros.

Is there more than meets the eye to this Hispanic gorilla? He could not help but wonder at that moment, but then dismissed the thought when a quick glance at the Poljot watch on his left wrist made him aware of the time. Shit! His date for the night was about to show up, and he was still tied up with Leo and his problems....

"You believe you did the right thing, Leo?" He grunted, but there was anger and frustration welling up in his chest and the Russian felt he was on the verge of losing his temper. "Listen up, *cabrón*, with the kind of bread I'm paying you and your freaking minions I can afford to fire you guys tonight and hire another crew by tomorrow morning!"

Leo knew he must take the chewing, and he did so like a man. That was one of the hardships one had to put up with when you're in middle management; you serve as a "cushion" between the *gran jefe* and the *peones*. Pavenko took a deep breath and a long sip from his drink, the vodka calmed him down.

"Look, just make sure those sons of bitches you hired don't fuck up again," he said in a harsh tone, "and the same goes for you, *cabrón*! You dig?"

Leo swallowed hard and rushed to nod his head. "Yes, boss. Don't you worry about my men. This won't happen again. I give you my word."

"What are you going to do with the corpse? You can't keep it in the apartment...."

"Not planning to, boss. I'll have it dumped in the river tonight, but I'm going to need a new car; that's the main reason why I came to see you. Can you get us one? It must be a stolen vehicle."

Yuri sighed again, so many complications all of a sudden precisely in such a promising evening, when Mirta had agreed to meet him at the disco....

"Okay," he said, "you call Turk and let him get you one... Will that be all?"

"Yes, boss. Sorry to have bothered you," answered Leo, but before he finished the phrase, the big man realized that the Russian had stopped paying him attention.

Pavenko had turned around in his stool to watch the fascinating walk of a gorgeous brunette passing by the bar in a short, red dress that stuck like a second skin to her curvy figure.

The newcomer took a table for two near the dance floor, but before she sat down the woman waved a hand at the Russian operative and flashed a disarming smile to the fortunate Slav.

"Wow!" Leo exclaimed. "You know that chick?"

The KGB agent grinned. "Yeah," he said, "she is an acquaintance..." then he turned very seriously and snapped at Leo. "Don't waste any more time and go see Turk, Leo. You need to have a vehicle ready for our next pick up. I'll call you later to see how it went."

"Sure, boss. Relax! Hope you have fun."

His last words were underlined by sarcasm, but Pavenko ignored them. Leo turned his back on the Russian and began to walk away. However, having seen the beautiful stranger stirred some unnerving thoughts in Balmaseda's mind. He turned around and — after putting some distance between them — stared at the woman once more, before abandoning the disco for good. He did not feel surprised to find her sitting next to the Russian, chatting, and drinking very enthusiastically.

Shit, he thought, *where have I seen her before?*

*C*hapter *12*

THOSE LITTLE SECRETS

Sometime later that very same evening, a maroon Ford van entered the Queens apartment building's parking lot. Leo was behind the wheel. After driving around one side of the edifice, looking for a convenient place to park, he lucked out and found a spot right behind the apartment where the safehouse was set up. He killed the engine and got out of the van. He stuck his right hand in the trench coat pocket and brought out a flat automatic camera with a built-in flash bulb. Leo checked the gizmo, made sure it was loaded with a fresh roll of film, and returned it to its place of origin. There was a satisfaction grin distorting his mouth as he walked toward the building's main entrance.

However, in the back of his mind, the memory of the gorgeous brunette he'd seen at the salsa disco in Pavenko's company kept hammering his brain.

Jesus, he couldn't stop thinking, *what a sexy bitch!*

When Mack Dempsey heard the knocking at the door, he immediately alerted Lucas. This time they were both prepared; they got up quickly from the sofa facing the door and withdrew their weapons. The huge redhead crossed the space separating him from the door in complete silence, and his movements had the grace of a smaller man of lesser weight. He stopped to one side only a couple of feet from the door and looked at his buddy. Lucas had positioned himself in a kitchen angle, his Browning Hi-Power aimed at the entrance.

"Who is calling?" shouted Mack.

"C'mon, boys, open the door! It's me, Leo!"

Mack recognized his boss's voice and, without letting his guard down, took a step forward to unlatch the door. After that he regained his position with the gun at the ready.

"Come in!" he shouted.

Leo opened the door and did as he was told, careful not to make any sudden moves. The minute he turned to face Mack the redhead placed the barrel of his massive .357 magnum against the New York Rican's forehead.

"Easy, Candy, put that cannon away. You guys did it by the book this time." Leo waited for his man to holster the weapon and watched that Lucas, who was coming out of the kitchen holding the Browning, did the same. "In fact, you guys have a little fun-time coming, but first I need you to run an errand for me. Get the corpse in the tub wrapped up in plastic, weigh it down and dump it in the East River. When you are done, take the rest of the night off. Here, go have some fun, dudes!"

He took out a wad of bills from one of his pants pockets and peeled off a couple of hundreds, handing one to each man.

"It's on the house, okay?"

When the two mercs saw their boss smiling, they nodded, pocketed the dough, and went to work. Leo helped them get the dead man in the back of the van, bid them farewell and returned to the apartment. He locked himself in and took out the camera with the built-in flash.

He was grinning deviously while murmuring to himself: "Okay, friend Yuri, let's find out what is your little
secret."

*C*hapter *13*

THE FOX AND THE BEAR

Meanwhile, in Mirta's Jackson Heights apartment, the Cuban Mata Hari and her Russian partner were all over each other, kissing fiercely. They were sitting on the living room couch, and Pavenko was already in the absorbing process of undressing her.

"Jesus, you are smoking *hot* tonight!" breathed the brunette pulling away a little.

"I'm *dying* to screw you, woman," he grumbled.

Struggling to get him off her, Mirta sat up and smoothed out the dress that the Russian had already pulled all the way up to her hips. Then she walked briskly toward the cabinet's bar.

"Oh, we'll have some sex tonight, sweetie," she assured him. "But I need a stiff drink first. Want one?"

Pavenko sighed deeply and suppressed the desire he felt to run after her, throw her on the floor and rape her right there and then.

"All right, make it a vodka tonic, then — if you have vodka."

"I'll fetch it right away," said Mirta, smiled and started rummaging around in the cabinet's bar. "By the way, who was that big man back at the disco?"

The Russian looked at her quizzically. "What man?"

he inquired.

"The bouncer-type you were chatting with when I arrived; he undressed me with his eyes."

"Ah, you mean Leo," he said and smiled. "Why do you ask, are you interested?

"Are you out of your freakin' mind, Yuri? That guy gave me the creeps! He looked so morbid and ape-like; who is he?"

"Bah, don't worry about him, he's just some un-scrupulous shamus. *Nothing* to do with you."

Mirta nodded and returned to the sofa with the drinks. She settled down next to the Russian and passed him one. Pavenko's answer annoyed her, she was always suspicious of people who "had nothing to do with her."

"Drink," she said, raising her glass to toast. "Cheers!"

After clinking glasses, Pavenko toasted: "To a long night of sex and vodka!"

They drank and set the empty vessels aside. Pavenko embraced her and she, much to her regret, forced herself to do much more than let herself be screwed. She had received orders from Moscow and had to exploit the weakness Yuri had for her. She unbuttoned his pants and after caressing his organ with her hands, she put it in her mouth and began to work on him with well-contained disgust. Mirta was lesbian, and her intention was to appease the Russian with her lips without getting as far as a full vaginal penetration, but during the scuffle that she would lose along with all clothes, the Cuban-born Soviet agent could not suppress a thought:

A private detective, huh?

Nearly an hour later, once the best saboteur of the Ato-mic Fang Division had all the fun he could stand with his lady friend's superb body (something the beautiful woman fought in vain to avoid), they were both lying naked on the carpet not far from the couch, exhausted, when Yuri surprised her with an unexpected inquiry:

"Tell me why, Mirta?"

"Uh? Why what?" she asked, turning to look him in the eye.

"Why did you do it, do you think I'm not aware of what your sexual preferences are? I've read your file, baby. Why did you indulge me, Mirta? Are you in some kind of trouble that you can't handle with the Center, and need my support?"

Mirta didn't answer that for a moment; Yuri's question had taken her by surprise; she restrained herself from throwing in his face that the one who was in trouble with the Directorate was *him*; would he suspect that they were trying to control him through her charms? Would he be furious about that?

"Perceptive, aren't you? Why didn't you ask before screwing me? You'd have saved me the hard time I've been having!"

Yuri laughed helplessly, his harsh, deep laughter detonated by the bitterness reflected in the voice of the woman, who had ostensibly shed the mask and no longer pretended to be a nymph for his exclusive pleasure.

"You know how long I've been longing for your body, baby?"

Her body was every man's dream, and she knew it. But even though, she thought well about what she was going to say next before speaking. "Are you hinting that, since you have already indulged yourself, you've satisfied all your desires? I don't interest you anymore?"

Yuri understood that it was now the moment when he should be most wary about what they talked about. The vulnerability of a human male — any man, mind you —

increases considerably right after sexual intercourse. This is always the moment when the female of the species makes her move to impose whatever conditions she may have thought of earlier in the game, and thus begins the process of manipulation.

"I prefer to listen to your motives before answering that; it is clear to me that what just transacted here between us is a trade, isn't it?" Then he pulled her close to him and tenderly kissed one of her breasts. "What's wrong with you, Mirta?" He whispered in her ear, in a voice with paternal overtones. The lasciviousness that moments before had predominated in him had vanished.

Almost two minutes passed during which the only audible sound in the room was the elaborate breathing of those two beings. Then Mirta emitted a muffled moan followed by her best actress tears. She wept silently, languidly, seemingly devoid of passion but full of grief.

"They trust no one, Yuri..." she moaned, "they have no consideration for anyone. What would you think if I told you that I've had enough, that I'm fed up with all this?"

"What exactly does that mean?"

"You damn well know what it means! I am tired of pretending to be something I am not, of being a KGB whore!!"

The last was hissed with restrained rage. Such vehemence in her words frightened the Russian for a moment; Mirta didn't seem to be pretending.

"They trust no one, coño..." she muttered, "they have no consideration for anyone. I want out!!"

"For God's sake, woman, are you serious?"

"Yes! Though I'm sure the word lesbian is on my file, my pimps in the Directorate S keep ordering me to sleep with men whenever it's required during an operation, repeatedly, as if I enjoy it! It's not enough that I gave up my former position with the American Department of my own country's Intelligence service to collaborate with you people; it's not enough that I risk my neck watching over the operations of your illegal agents, like you! *Nothing* is ever enough!"

She paused for effect, giving time to her lament to get to the Russian. "I've had enough, damn it, I want *out* of this shit!"

"Don't even think about it, Mirta, don't even say it as a joke. You know for a fact that we're all doomed to serve until the end. They'll kill you."

"Maybe not... Remember that I don't have the same hierarchy as you in this game; I'm not an important piece on the board."

"Oh, but you're wrong. You also play a relevant role in this mission. Besides, you know too much to be allowed to walk away alive...."

"Yeah? That's what you say now, but if you knew what I know, it would be a different story. Maybe you'd even help me to vanish and come with me. *Together* we can make it!"

"Are you serious, Mirta? What's gotten into you?"

She held his gaze defiantly; the time had come to give the final blow to the bull in front of her.

"They don't trust you, Yuri. I've been ordered to stick to you like a hanger-on, to keep an eye on you. That's why I've been compelled to have sex with you! You wanted to know why; there, now you know!"

After a brief pause to let the weight of her words cause the desired effect, she wrapped it up in a tone as quiet as it was grim:

"They fear that this current mission of yours — whatever it might be — will make your knees shake at the moment of truth."

Chapter 14

DOUBLE PLAY

Somewhat dismayed by the events of the previous evening — the impact of the news Mirta had broken to him — Yuri Pavenko left the Jackson Heights flat where his colleague dwelled and went about his daily business, whatever that might be. Most likely to prepare the conditions for the next pick-up at the Manhattan pier.

As soon as he'd left, Mirta breathed a sigh of relief and jumped out of bed. In a jiffy she bathed and then dressed, taking great care to regain a seductive appearance, for she was to meet another man who also found her irresistible and whom she was considering manipulating into assisting her with the dirty work. We already know that her mission for the KGB was to look after Pavenko's operation from the outside, even if she didn't know, exactly, what his task consisted of.

Before leaving her flat, she made a phone call that took her next victim by surprise, as the guy had already lost track of her for quite some time. The fella who answered the call was named Emilio Furias (a compatriot of hers) a former colleague from the General Intelligence Directorate who was also a militant in the ranks of the *Departamento América* of the Cuban DGI.

The morning was grey and rainy, with an annoying

little wind ruffling the lapels of her raincoat as she waited for Emilio, standing by the main entrance of Trinity Church, at the intersection of Broadway and Wall Street, an area known as Lower Manhattan.

It was a typical wet autumn day in New York, and the throng of human beings that swarmed the wet asphalt streets, like Mirta, also protected themselves from the rain and the wind with all sorts of umbrellas, hats, rubber capes and waterproof jackets. Some passed by her with their faces buried deep in their lapels, heading for different destinations, while others were just trying to survive another day in the Big Apple. The annoying little wind ruffled the chokers of her raincoat as she impatiently waited for Emilio, standing by the main entrance of Trinity Church, at the intersection of Broadway and Wall Street, an area known as Lower Manhattan. Mirta was wearing sunglasses and a scarf on her head, even though the daylight made her conspicuous by its weakness, but her restless eyes, hidden behind dark lenses, scanned the crowd that swarmed around her searching for a familiar face.

Where the hell are you, Emilio? she thought, pacing restlessly in front of the church doors. *You should be here by now!*

But at that very moment her ever-vigilant eyes spotted Mr. Furias crossing the street, and a relieved smile tugged at her lips. The guy had kept his word. If he had dropped everything and run to see her it was an obvious sign that he was still interested in her....

Emilio was, believe me.

The man who came to her side was short in stature but seemed to be in great shape. He possessed a well-muscled, sinewy body, and moved with the feline grace of a Martial Arts practitioner. He was probably a Judo fighter; Cuban agents excelled at that. Emilio had white, leathery skin, pretty much like an Anglo-Saxon, and his hair was a very light brown, almost blond. He could pass well for a gringo until you heard him speak: His English had a slight accent. The file said he was in his early thirties.

As he approached, Mirta watched him closely and concluded that the trench coat, the parasol, and attaché briefcase he was carrying gave him the appearance of a New York stock exchange executive. What a great disguise! But, make no mistake, Mirta Alicia Velasco, who'd known Emilio Furias well in her time with the America Department, was aware that she was dealing with a vulgar and pernicious creature; the man was one of those Soviet-trained assassins that the DGI took to sending abroad to serve in dangerous missions.

The man got to her side, also flashing a complacent grin, and they embraced and kissed each other on the cheeks. Then they held hands, like a couple of lovers, and began to walk away from the church down Wall Street, merging into the dense pedestrian traffic of the area.

"So, you're still working with the *bolos*, eh?" said Emilio, referring to the Russians by their Cuban-given nickname, "you're really missed in the Department, *chica*. After you left us, nothing is the same."

"Ah, come on, don't be a toady. I miss those days too, you know. That's the truth."

"It's a real shame you're not coming back with us. Now the ones taking your place are skinny malnourished girls who strive to look like those skinny American fashion models from the magazines."

A brief pause to look her up and down, without hiding his lasciviousness.

"I must confess that even I would go to work for the *bolos*, if that would get you to open your legs for me...."

Mirta looked him in the eye and pursed her lips. The thought of it made her stomach churn, but that was exactly why she'd come to meet him, and the fact that Emilio still lusted after her gave her a sense of relief, which mitigated her displeasure.

"You know, now that you mention it, that's where this it's going," she said with a mellifluous smile.

"I knew it," said Emilio, "who do I have to kill, baby?"

They both laughed at his last words, but Mirta didn't doubt for a moment that the man was serious.

"I just want you to help me identify someone. I need an expert in surveillance and photography; that's your thing, isn't it?"

"What about the *bolos*, don't they have anyone with those qualifications? Don't fuck with me, Mirta; this is New York! Those bastards have a consulate here!"

But the woman's face hardened, and she snapped at her companion: "That's precisely the problem, Emilio! I can't count on the local *Rezidentura,* I'm working strictly with the illegals, I need an outsider like you. A *compañero,* someone I can trust! Are you interested or not? I didn't come here to play games."

Emilio didn't like the drastic variation of her attitude, but he knew how women change when they think they're not going to get away with what they want, so he let it go. In any case, he was interested in balling her. If a *yanqui* — that's Spanish for Yank — or a *bolo* had to die to accomplish his goal, it didn't matter... not if it remained a secret between them and it didn't reach his superiors' ears.

"All right, *chica*, okay. Calm down now." He looked into her eyes with uncaring intensity, before speaking again. "I'll do what you ask if it doesn't go against the interests of the Department. But I want your full body in return. Promise me you'll do anything I desire."

Mirta was not daunted by his fierce stare; she too was tough; she held his gaze and hissed: "Deal!"

And with her dry, carefully articulated reply, the Cuban spy named Mirta Alicia Velasco condemned her buddy Emilio to die a violent death. Of course, neither of them was aware of it at the time.

Chapter 15

OVERSIGHTS AND MISGIVINGS

A couple of days later, Leo was walking briskly down Broadway Street when he stopped suddenly by a public phone booth. Those following him at a safe distance did the same, and as P.I. Balmaseda entered the cubicle they photographed him with a zoom scope. Completely unaware that he was being spied on, Leo lifted the receiver and placed some coins in the narrow slot of the metal box. When he got a clear line, he dialed a certain Washington, D.C. number.

After three rings, someone answered the call at the other end of the line.

Leo cleared his throat and said: "The code name is Landon. I'm calling from Manhattan, need to talk to the Colonel, please; it's urgent."

That same night, my boss flew over to Manhattan. In my opinion that was a mistake, but it happened during our formative period when the Quadrille was still a long way from being nearly as efficient as it eventually became.

At that time, Marlon Berkowitz did not yet have the resources or the organization that we later came to have, once we proved to the top brass of our Department of Defense the importance of keeping a peacetime

Counterintelligence operation — like ours, naturally — running behind the scenes. Unfortunately, agents of all levels and ranks fail at some point in their careers. Even the most experienced, as was the case with William Buckley, for instance, a legend in the history of the CIA. Buckley fell into a death trap in the most foolish way, while leaving his Beirut flat, in Lebanon, and was captured by Islamic jihadist terrorists. This cost him a long and painful year of physical and mental torture that culminated in his death.

Another time, a group of veteran U.S. Secret Service agents failed to stop John Hinckley, Jr. when he tried for President Reagan's life. So, if my boss hadn't shown up at Landon's Jackson Heights apartment, things would have gone smoother for us. But just as it had happened with Leo, he also was marked.

The Colonel took one of the photographs on the coffee table and examined it closely.

"Hum, very interesting... Where did you get these pictures, Landon?"

The two of them were sharing the couch in the living room of the flat. Leo frowned and grimaced.

"A few months ago, I met a client; a Russian named Yuri."

"Yuri? You know his surname?"

"Negative, sir; I met the fella through a small-time crook who goes by the name of Turk. The Russian introduced himself to me as a dealer looking for protection, but it was never clear what he is distributing. At first, I thought it was drugs, which is common in these days of feverish cocaine consumption. In any case, what I do know is that the merchandise has been arriving by sea. On the first day of every month, my boys and I escort Yuri to the Seaport Mall on South Street and make sure no one disturbs him while we pick up a package. We then escort him back to his safehouse and stand guard there for the rest of the month, until the routine is repeated."

The Colonel returned the photo to the center table and tilted his head to look at Leo.

"You say this Yuri has a safehouse?"

"Yes, sir, he does. I set it up for him."

"Where?"

"In the borough of Queens."

"How many little trips to the harbor is that now?"

"The next one will be my fifth."

"And you still think he's dealing drugs?"

Landon scratched his head before answering the question.

"No, sir, I don't; see, those engravings in Cyrillic next to the handle of the briefcases have changed my mind. That's why you're here."

"Worrisome, aren't they?"

At his boss's bitter smile, Leo (a.k.a. Agent Landon) pulled a handkerchief from his pocket and blew his nose.

"There's something else, Colonel," before Leo continued, he produced a picture from his coat pocket and held it in front of the Colonel's eyes, "does this gal looks familiar to you?"

The Colonel took the photo and studied it for a few seconds. Then shook his head.

"No, I don't think so, why?"

"My old bloodhound instinct tells me that this broad is no mere bystander."

"That's why you took the picture, huh?"

Leo nodded his head. "I saw her with Yuri at a disco, but she could be an expensive call girl for all I know; she looks like it. However, I want you to circulate her image and see if you can find a match in the FBI's Counterintelligence Division files. Please, do it ASAP, will you?"

The Colonel put the picture away and nodded. "All right."

"If you find out anything, let me know immediately. I have a hunch that this woman works for someone; if we find out who that is, we can fit her into the puzzle."

The Colonel nodded approvingly, sat back, picked up all the other pics on the table and tucked them in his attaché.

"Well, it looks like you've stumbled into something that merits our attention here; good work, Landon. I'll be leaving now. I must be back in Washington tonight. I'll get the photos of the briefcases to the CIA's Department of Science & Technology. In the meantime, keep an eye on the Russian for us; I'm sending someone to take care of the woman."

The night Mirta chose to take out her bitterness on Yuri, a whole world of uncertainty and resentment was born inside the Soviet agent. He was so perplexed at what he'd been told that he didn't know how to react. He barely managed to leave her flat in a hassled manner, without voicing a single word about it again, neither for nor against. Quite understandable if you ask me, but it was not to stay that way. Mirta had taken a good gamble and soon the cancer of doubt began to gnaw at Yuri's insides. Had he been secretly ostracized from the Party's elite?

One Sunday afternoon he turned up at the Cuban woman's apartment unannounced. The whiff of vodka wafting from his bulky body was enough for anyone in his vicinity to realize that the Russian had been drinking. Not one to mince words, he approached the woman and grabbed her by the shoulders almost violently.

"Tell me who suspects me!" he roared.

Mirta looked at him with great apprehension but did not dare to tell him.

"Tell me, damn it!" Yuri shouted again, and this time he unceremoniously grabbed her with both hands.

"Who are your Moscow contacts!"

She realized then that perhaps she'd gone too far; Pavenko was determined to get to the bottom of the matter. She had to throw him a bone to calm him down and then, of course, turn him around little by little until she had him eating out of her palm. This was the strategy that had always worked better for her with men: sex and manipulation.

Soviet Russia was always noted for being a gigantic breeding ground for paranoid entities, from the highest Party leader to the lowliest and most insignificant of its citizens. Communism is a system that thrives on fear, suspicion, hunger, and deception, and so entrenches itself in you until it entirely dominates your soul. That afternoon, the most dangerous illegal agent the KGB had in all of New York proved that even *he* was not immune to that formula.

Mirta tried to master the fear she felt welling up inside and let out a sigh. "My instructions are being radioed to me directly from Department V," she mumbled. "There is no specific name I can give you."

Yuri let her go, he didn't need to hear the name from Mirta's lips; he already knew who it was.

"Department V you say, hum," he muttered, "then it must be Major Kirov who doesn't trust me...."

He let go of Mirta and took a few steps across the room, until he stopped to wave his arms as if he intended to take flight: "Of course, it makes sense, you damned old son of a bitch!"

He turned to Mirta; his face contorted with spite.

"You know what I should do?'" He shouted bitterly, his hoarse voice shaking with rage. "I should wait until I have all the components together, and hand them over on a silver platter to the bloody FBI! That's what the stuffy bastards deserve!"

As Mirta had no idea that Pavenko was referring to a 10-kiloton atomic bomb, she did not feel the full weight of the threat. I'm sure she thought Yuri was referring to some other warlike techno gizmo the Soviets were out to steal from the Americans. Then she saw the opportunity to fulfil her role; this was the key moment to lasso the bull and bring it into the fold.

"Calm down, Yuri, please," she said in a tone as soft as it was sweet, "I'm on your side... Remember the other night at the salsa club, that oversized brute of a man in hat and coat conversing with you?"

Despite the red haze, produced by the effects of alcohol mixed with the rage that enveloped his brain, Pavenko stopped his bitching abruptly and stared at her with renewed interest.

"The shamus," added Mirta, "when I asked you who he was that night, you answered that he was a shamus. Do you remember?"

"Leo Balmaseda...." Yuri hissed.

"Is that his name?"

"By that name I know him, what about him? Do you know something about Leo that I should know?'

"As far as knowing for sure, can't say I do, but, seeing him there with you gave me a bad feeling. Be wary of that man, Yuri, keep an eye on him without letting him notice. Perhaps he's one of us sent by Directorate S for a purpose that neither you nor I know anything about. Or he may be an American agent for all I know."

Mirta's last words had a strange effect on the KGB

man. The "angry bear" who had a few minutes earlier burst into her flat, pawing at her, transformed into a "cunning fox."

In the long run, this would turn out to have stern consequences for Agent Landon, which is why I always say that where many men fail, a woman prevails.

Chapter 16

CODE NAME DELTA

During the five months following my enlistment in the Quadrille, I perfected many of the techniques I had learned with the Rangers and cultivated a few new ones. From my former status as a sniper, I was required to upgrade to the level of pistol competition marksman, which by Quadrille's standards meant averaging a *minimum* of two hundred hours per month of practice at the range — emphasis on the word minimum. The guns I practiced with varied in caliber, type, and make. I was forced to train with almost all domestic and some foreign brands. But at the end of the course, we were saddled with what the Colonel called "the weapon worthy of a true eliminator": a Smith & Wesson Mack 22, Model 0, 9-millimeter Parabellum pistol, also known as the Hush Puppy and manufactured exclusively in the good old U.S. of A. Before that intense training I'd always been a lover of the Colt .45 — the M1911A1 model if it matters — but the Hush Puppy changed me. It was a unique gun, really; only a few hundred ever went into production and almost all of them were distributed among our Special Forces during the Vietnam War, mostly because the slide could be locked and suppresses the sound of the shot as much as possible, something totally censored by the Geneva Convention.

They also turned me into a sailor and a pilot; by the time I finished there I was able to fly anything from a commercial helicopter to a four-seater light aircraft and pilot anything from a racing boat to a medium-sized yacht. I learned how to caper with all types of vehicles; how to avoid crashes, how to crash-car, how to minimize the damage in an unavoidable accident, how to escape unscathed from a motorized chase, how to shoot one-handed while driving with the other. In short, comparing my life back then to the safer but tedious routine of the barracks at Fort Benning, now I was having fun!

However, I couldn't say the same for the opposition: for those Communist agents infiltrating New York, things were about to start getting complicated....

One cloudless night, nearing the end of the fifth month of training, the Colonel gathered us all together in the Operations Room of our Washington headquarters, a gloomy eleven-story building that stood on the banks of the Anacostia River. We were twenty recruits in all, men and women of various ethnic backgrounds and walks of life, but at heart we all were as white, red, and blue as the very flag we were sworn to defend. Marlon Berkowitz introduced us to a guy from Boston named Tilson who was supposed to be a "wet works" specialist, the Colonel said; this Tilson had served more than five years with the CIA's Moscow Section. He told us this man would teach us how to kill, in cold blood and upon demand; Tilson would also lecture us on this new enemy we were all being sent out to stop.

The ex-CIA master-assassin explained that this was a

peculiar opponent, not the typical henchman of the Soviet secret police or the common Warsaw Pact soldiery. This was a very special enemy, well-trained and motivated, the spearhead of the infamous KGB. They were the elite shadow warriors of the Soviet underground. Therefore, we had to learn the assassin's trade, and learn it well, because those whom we would be sent out to track down and neutralize were also highly trained nuclear saboteurs and murderers.

After an extensive and interesting preparatory speech, in which he compared killing on demand to a sublime form of art, where it's necessary to envision and plan the action thoroughly before performing it, he gave us a practical exercise: to select and execute *four* opposition agents, in cold blood, thus discarding the use of firearms, edged weapons, or explosives.

And he asked us just to use our imagination.

The last thing the man told us that night was that, in North America, the KGB espionage apparatus was composed of an official cadre of resident agents, or *Rezidentura*, of Soviet origin, and a band of illegal agents, of mixed nationalities, among which the Cuban operatives of the DGI stood out. He compared the Cubans with the Gurkha soldiers used by the British and with the Bulgarian mercenaries who did the dirty work of the KGB in Eastern and Western Europe, giving as an example the most recent plot in Rome, an attempt on the life of one Karol Wojtyla, otherwise known as Pope John Paul II.

That same cloudless night, when I was most engrossed in selecting my targets, I received an urgent call from my boss, summoning me to his office in an hour, where I was ordered to prepare a suitcase with a couple of changes of clothes and the essential toiletries for travel. When, already prepared, I walked into his office, the Colonel assigned me a code name (Delta), withdrew me from the collective exercise assigned by Tilson and surprisingly changed my status from that of unit recruit to full-time eliminator of the Quadrille, with a mission.

Two hours later, still half-stunned by the abruptness with which things had transpired, I was landing at La Guardia Airport in New York.

Chapter 17

NEW YORK, NEW YORK

Arriving in the Big Apple, I set out to look at the possible scenarios where I would be operating — or, at least, expected to. The dossier Marlon Berkowitz had given me to study during the flight pointed to four different locations, but Landon had indicated that the final battle would be fought on the South Street Seaport Mall in Lower Manhattan, at the pier in the harbor where the merchant ship carrying the bomb components always arrived. Nevertheless, I decided to move around and get acquainted with most of the city.

I took a taxi ride through Time Square, drove through Central Park, toured the Meat Packing District, Greenwich Village and even Madison Square Garden. But I soon became convinced that the real theatre of operations for my first mission with the Quadrille, as Landon had pointed out, would be the Seaport Mall. Nonetheless, a funny thing happened: The whole time the tour was going on, I kept "listening" in my head to the voice of Frank Sinatra singing:

If I can make it there, I'll make it anywhere....

And to be honest, I went to bed that night praying that the old *maestro* wasn't wrong.

"What have you been able to find out?" Mirta asked bluntly once they met again at the corner of the church.

By that time, she had already seen the photos Emilio had taken of Leo and my boss together during the Colonel's visit to Jackson Heights and had given the order to her former colleague in the *Departamento América* to investigate them thoroughly.

"I need to know who that big hairy ape and the bald chimpanzee in the picture really are. I know I've seen their ugly mugs somewhere before."

"Probably so," Emilio agreed, "they are booked in our archives. I'm surprised the *bolos* don't have them in theirs."

"Don't be, there are many things we know that they still don't," Mirta said, referring to the Russians.

"That man you're interested in, the bald guy, he's a tough customer. He's an old-school pro, we came across him for the first time in Vietnam."

"Seriously?"

"Oh, yes. Then we tracked him down in Granada, during the invasion."

"Wow... And who is he?"

"In Nam he was a captain with the U.S. Navy SEALs. By the way, that big ape, as you call him, was there with him too. He was part of his assault group. Then baldie started overseeing joint Special Forces operations that involved the Army Rangers, the Green Berets and the Air Force as well, and he was transferred from the Navy and promoted to a full colonel for Special Services."

Emilio paused and spat on the sidewalk.

"Grenada was a bit different," he continued, "the little colonel didn't show his face there, but he made his presence felt from a post with the U.S. Southern Command. We think he was the brain behind the operations of an elite group of snipers totally dedicated to eliminating our best officers on the island. He hit us hard, you know, we lost some good men because of him. I mean if it was really him."

"Gee, that's *very* interesting, what does he do now?"

"Operations; there are rumors that he has become a non-killing assassin, a 'Black bag' strategist, although no one knows what new group he commands and what exactly for. But what everyone agrees on is that the guy is a formidable tactician and always operates from the shadows with a concise unit of select fighters."

"For God's sake, do you know his name?"

"Yes, I do. His name is Marlon Berkowitz, Col. Marlon Berkowitz, U.S. Special Forces, Ret."

"And the gorilla?"

"First name Leo, last name Balmaseda. Born in New York City of Puerto Rican parents. He is a private investigator licensed to practice in the state of New York. Believed to have a shady past, connections with the Italian and Irish mafia, you know. He frequents the pubs of Hell's Kitchen."

"I see, so they know each other from back in the day," Mirta said. "Do you think there's still a military connection between them?"

Emilio shrugged his shoulders: "I haven't the slightest idea, *muñeca*, but if you find out anything, let us know."

"Sure, right away."

"And now tell me, doll, are you satisfied? If so, I'd like you to keep your part of the bargain. Now."

This happened on the very day of my arrival in New York, so when I visited Agent Landon at his Jackson Heights flat that night, on the Colonel's orders, I was marked by the opposition.

In all honesty, I never felt very comfortable with the idea of meeting Landon at his own den, but I also thought that if he was being watched and we were caught together elsewhere, the result would be the same, wouldn't it? Perhaps my showing up so naively at his apartment would disconcert the enemy a bit.

I was wrong.

Conferring with Leo, I learned that Yuri Pavenko had scheduled another pick-up at the harbor in a couple of days. The action was to take place at Pier 16, ETA 0300 hours.

On the second day of my arrival in Manhattan, unaware that one faction of the enemy cell had already identified Leo and the Colonel as "enemies in action," I set about the task of eliminating the illegal agents who were supporting the Soviet operation. It was also a way of avoiding feeling guilty about dodging the practical exercise Tilson had assigned all recruits during our training in Maryland; I would kill them all by his rules: no guns, no edged weapons, no explosives... I would only use my imagination, right?

At least, those were my intentions.

Unaware that Mirta and Emilio had also noticed me, I bumped into them as they pretended to walk hand in hand down Broadway. We left Trinity Church behind and arrived separately at her flat in Jackson Heights, which was not far from Leo's apartment. As I had observed them walking around in a very amorous mood, I gave them time to get well into their erotic games before I raided the apartment. Don't forget that I am an eliminator and that when I'm activated it's because there are no more diplomatic avenues left to achieve the desired objective — whatever it might be.

I entered the Jackson Heights flat through the bathroom window, thinking I was clever and ready for anything, without even suspecting that I had stepped into a trap. Emilio finished undressing her — I could see everything from my position, through the crack of the bathroom's half-open door — and ordered her to get on all fours on the sofa. They were in the living room, where Pavenko had sat with her the night the Cuban Mata Hari had decided to use her bodily charms on the Russian agent in compliance with her orders from Moscow.

"What are you up to?" Mirta asked with a hint of apprehension in her voice, but she submitted to her companion's demand and knelt on the sofa seat, resting her bare breasts and forearms on the back of the furniture.

"You said that if I helped you in this case, you'd let me do whatever I want with your body, didn't you?

She tilted her head to look at him out of the corner of her eye and answered: "Yes, that's what I said," but her voice still harbored that tone of reserve which began to cause an effervescent expectation in me and triggered the alarm system in my self-preservation instinct.

"I can't wait to screw you doggy style, baby" hissed Emilio and stood facing the woman's back. "Come on, *chica*, get your ass up, *mulata rica*... You don't know how long I've been longing to fuck you like this!"

"Emilio...."

"Shut up and obey, cunt!"

The scene was becoming more and more seductive, especially for a young red-blooded male in his early twenties, to whom the last five months of very intense training with a band of government assassins, had left him no time for anything else but learning the trade of "the fifth profession."

"You brute!" Mirta shouted and soon Emilio was panting, grumbling, and grunting, and she was shrieking, cursing him in a strained voice choked with the effort, and moaning in a calculatedly plaintive tone embellished with certain erotic gruffy sounds that I found too stimulating, regardless of the situation. They pretended to copulate, but as I approached the sofa on my tiptoes, Mirta tilted her body and pushed Emilio aside. Before I knew what was happening, the naked woman was pointing a light, semi-auto pistol at my face — probably a .22 — that she must have kept hidden beneath the cushions of the love seat.

I reacted by slapping her armed hand with my right, which deflected the barrel of the gun to the left, right at the moment of the shot and Emilio lost an ear. Then I snatched the little pistol away from Mirta and shot him dead. She took advantage of the moment of my distraction with her partner to jump on me, and almost clawed out my right eye with her pointed fingernails. I threw her over my shoulder and, as she fell, I crushed her right hand with a stomp. The bones in her hand creaked pitifully, but she didn't let out a sound. Oh, she was a tough one! Mirta clamped down on my legs and knocked me down. I rolled on top of her, my eye bleeding profusely now, and managed to straddle her bare bust.

Putting my weight on both my knees I pinned her arms down first and then I strangled her.

*C*hapter *18*

THE PARTY IS OVER

On the next night Landon decided that we should close the operation and between the two of us we took the Queens hideout. We killed the mercenaries guarding the Russian's safehouse and waited for the arrival of Pavenko, who was supposed to show up after midnight. During the time it took the KGB agent to show up, Landon gave me the details on how they collected the bomb components, which arrived in metal suitcases that looked like an attaché. He also warned me about a gigantic merchant seaman (presumably a Soviet agent) who delivered the goods to Pavenko at Pier 16 of the wharf, where the Russian cargo ship was docked. Hearing agent Landon call the Soviet sailor "gigantic" worried me; Landon was not exactly a man of ordinary stature....

That night Yuri decided to go back to the Latin salsa disco, he had been giving a lot of thought to what he'd talked about with Mirta and wanted to see her again. As he didn't wish to compromise her further, in case of retaliation from her masters if the Cuban Mata Hari opted to do something crazy by defecting on her own, he decided not to visit her flat. He would meet her at the *discoteca*, a place often frequented by both. But Mirta didn't show up, and seeing that time was running out, he decided to take a gamble and made his way to Jackson Heights. He took a cab to the woman's place and when he rapped at the right door, expecting to hear her voice asking who was knocking, nothing happened.

A few seconds passed without any response to his knocking. With a gloomy foreboding throbbing in his heart, he pulled out a set of lock picks from a pocket and picked the lock. He entered and closed the door behind him. The room was dim and sunk in complete silence, but the stench of death that hit him full in the nostrils confirmed that he had arrived too late. From the waistband of his trousers, under a leather blazer, he pulled out a flat pistol and clutched it firmly in hand. He found Mirta's body on the carpet, not far from the love seat, next to that of a stranger. Both corpses were naked. The man had been shot more than once. Mirta had been strangled. A dull rage seized him, and he lost his temper. He started kicking at the furniture, but after a while he calmed down and, adopting a more professional attitude, Pavenko set about searching the flat thoroughly for clues. It didn't take him long to find one; it was in the bedroom, a Manila envelope resting on the bedside table next to the bed. Yuri took the sachet and ripped it open, emptying its contents onto the mattress. Scattered across the bed were all the photos taken by the late Emilio.

That's how Yuri Pavenko came to discover Leo conferencing with the Colonel — and, also with me.

When the man from the Atomic Fang Division knocked on the door of the Queens safehouse, it was after 01:30.

Landon motioned for me to go hide in the kitchen, but when he opened the door, the raging Russian pushed the barrel of his strange pistol through the crack and rested the business end of the gun on his head. It was an old Tula Tokarev, Model TT-33, one of those that went into production during the late 1920s, probably smuggled in through the New York docks. The Model TT-33 is nothing more than Soviet copy of the American Colt Government Model M1911, although the round it fires is the 7.62 millimeters one and not the robust .45 ACP cartridge like its Gringo counterpart, but it was an excellent and reliable weapon, mind you, thus it is still being manufactured under license in countries like Poland and North Korea.

Anyway, Yuri was furious.

He threatened to shoot Landon in the head if he didn't confess the whole truth and at that moment, I had the opportunity to shoot him, but I didn't for fear of killing the bugger on the spot and then not being able to recover the sixth component of the bomb. If Pavenko did not show up at Pier 16 of the South Street Seaport Mall at three o'clock sharp that morning, the Slavic sailor would vanish with the briefcase and raise the alarm.

While I reflected about this, the Atomic Fang Division saboteur lost his patience and shot my partner at point-blank range. I reacted by showing my face and firing at him with the Hush Puppy, but I didn't shoot to kill, of course, my intention was only to wound him. When the 9 mm slug went into his lower abdomen, the Russian howled like a coyote at the moon and fired back in my direction, forcing me to duck. By the time I was able to bring up my gun and aim it, the KGB man had vanished.

My first reaction was to assist Landon, but my wounded partner motioned me to ignore that for the moment and go after the saboteur. So, I left him there panting and grunting, and ran into the street. I took a taxi, which rushed me to the Brooklyn Bridge underpass, and then I walked along the bottom of the pier. Honest to God, I hated myself for leaving Landon wounded, but what could I do. With the Quadrille, closing the mission always came first. I walked with my nerves on edge, hands tucked deep into my trench coat pockets, looking everywhere for my fleeing target. Suddenly I spotted Yuri Pavenko's broad back, as he limped along the plank leading to the anchorage. I stayed behind, and followed him very cautiously now, as I still didn't know for sure if this was a trap; it all seemed too easy. Pavenko was clutching his wound with one hand and trudging forward. If my shot hadn't pierced one of his vital organs, it could take a man in his physical condition up to three hours to die of a belly wound.

He crossed Pier 17, and I couldn't help thinking that if the Soviets had a sniper posted on the roof of the Fulton Fish Market building, I was a dead man. Nonetheless, I clamped my sphincter, and persevered.

Pavenko left Pier 16 behind and lurched towards Pier 15, the first in line at the jetty. At that moment I knew he intended to ambush me, but determined to take him down anyway, I ran after him. When I reached the only place where an enemy could hide on the quay — the pilot house — instinct warned me, and I turned round. The Herculean sailor Landon had told me about was coming out of hiding and he tried to crush my skull with a heavy, metallic attaché case. I dodged it nimbly but lost my balance in the process and fell backwards onto the plank floor.

The blond colossus lifted the hefty metal case again, but my Hush Puppy was ready and waiting for him this time. I pulled the trigger four times in succession. The Slavic mammoth looked at his chest with incredulous eyes and collapsed. I felt footsteps and rolled over the plank and came up on one knee. Yuri Pavenko was running towards me now along the quay, shooting his bloody Tokarev one-handed and plugging the wound in his lower abdomen with the other. I realized that his gesture was futile, more generated by impotence and rage than a serious attempt to stop me — no shooter can aim a gun properly while simultaneously running and trying to stop a stomach hemorrhage — so I leaned my left elbow on one knee, steadied my breathing and shot him twice.

My mistake, according to the casefile, was that I didn't bother to finish him off; as far as I was concerned Pavenko was already done, just like his huge comrade on the dock. So, with my chest heaving with pride at completing my first assignment with the Quadrille, and my temples boiling with the excess adrenaline that combat generates, I reached for the briefcase containing the sixth component of the "dirty bomb" and shouted.

"Screw you all, motherfuckers! The party is over!"

And that was that.

*E*pilogue

Months later, after a slow recovery, Agent Landon was released from a Manhattan hospital, and he went back to his undercover duties. I was forced to return to Anacostia almost immediately after closing the mission and resume my training, this time working closely with Tilson, as soon as the Colonel reviewed the results of the Manhattan operation and decided that, although I was good agent material, I still lacked polish... At first — I confess — I was annoyed by his decision, but then I understood the logic of his actions and I even thanked him for it, my lone wolf nature allowed me to learn more and much faster by attending classes as the sole pupil of an ex-CIA grandmaster, than by participating in collective training. So it was that, several months later, I was sent on a secret mission to Moscow. That was the first time I set foot on the forbidden side of the Iron Curtain, when East and West were still divided.

Suddenly I found myself on a street in Central Moscow, on one of those mornings when the sun chooses to remain hidden, and a lot of muddy snow takes the opportunity to swirl everywhere. Wearing winter clothes (and with the skeleton of a dismantled sniper rifle cleverly packed and carried on my back in secret compartments of my bulky woolen overcoat), I walked up the street with both hands tucked deep in my pockets.

For a moment I paused to observe my contours, and when I saw no one following me, I looked up at the sparse block of buildings that rose across the street. At that precise moment the sun began to rise, and sunlight made me form a visor to protect my eyes with the back of my hands. I looked again, but seeing no one to stop me, I crossed the street in a shuffle towards the block of buildings. When I reached the first of the complex, Tilson left his hiding place and came out to meet me....

After reflecting long and hard on the incident, Col. Marlon Berkowitz had concluded that the Soviets' maneuver — introducing a portable atomic bomb in Manhattan — had been too daring an act to pass without a counterpunch. And it was, of course; on that we all agreed. The dilemma was how to strike back at the Reds without triggering World War III.

I still remember the look on his acerbic face the afternoon he met Tilson and me in his office to announce, rather enthusiastically for a man of his character: "I've got it!"

Tilson didn't say anything; neither did I. So, the Colonel went on.

"The idea came to mind while reading one of those Western pocketbooks. Don't laugh, gentlemen, I'm dead serious."

No one laughed, naturally, but his words generated a strained anticipation.

"A gunfight between two constables and ten rustlers, they face each other in a dusty alley; the constables stand with their backs to a wall, in front of them is the outlaw leader surrounded by his three fiercest cohorts, the remaining six rustlers gradually fall back."

I felt Tilson glance at me, so I tried to look back out of the corner of my eye, but when I did, I found him very focused on what the Colonel was saying and returned my attention to our superior.

"The most senior of the lawmen says to his partner in a loud voice, 'Everett, when I kill the gang leader and the gimp on the right, you take down the two on his left.' These constables were reputed to be both very quick with their guns and excellent marksmen; when the rest of the gang heard who would be the next in line, they became even more detached from the conflict....'"

Here he paused and looked at us. First at Tilson, his second in command, and then at me.

"Are you getting the picture? I'm going to assign you a target: the leader of the rustlers. Tilson, I want you to use your former resources at Moscow Section, the CIA must know who leads the KGB's Atomic Fang Division. It is that person we must eliminate. I don't care if it's a man or a woman. Let's get rid of the leader of the rustlers."

Then he turned to me:

"Delta, this will be your first assignment behind the Iron Curtain. Tilson will lead you to the mark, you know the drill. One shot, one kill."

The last phrase that escaped his mouth, as he addressed me that afternoon in his office in Anacostia, was the motto of the U.S. Marine snipers.

One shot, one kill.

No exceptions.

And now I was in Moscow, about to carry out his orders.

I began to climb the steps of the battered staircase leading to the third floor of the building; Tilson took the lift. Although our destination was the same, we had agreed to go up by different routes. I tried to remain composed for as long as it took me to reach the flat that concerned us, but it was no easy task, knowing that if I were caught in Moscow carrying a dismantled rifle, I would end up in the cold harsh dungeons of the ill-reputed Lubyanka prison. An unattractive prospect for a young American soldier of twenty-four, right? That's why I carried the infamous CIA "black pill" with me. One bite before I swallowed it and wham, the cyanide would spread across my tongue and take me out of my misery.

But they hadn't caught me yet and I had a job to do.

Tilson was already waiting at the end of the long corridor; as I began to walk leisurely towards the flat door, he did the same. We passed halfway, pretending not to know each other, but the quick silent look he gave me clearly said: *It's time.*

I didn't notice any symptoms of nervousness in him, he didn't look tense at all, but the man was a veteran in these matters — one of the best we had, mind you — and the terrain we were treading on was familiar to him. Moreover, his former CIA associates, having learned who the target was in this case and guessing that they would end up scoring the point by sheer weight of logic, agreed to facilitate the task without fully committing themselves. Well, who needed them?

Both Tilson and I had been supplied by the Moscow Section with Makarov pistols, the very same brand used by KBG officers, and fake credentials identifying us as members of the *Komitet*. But my Russian at that time was still macaronic; Tilson spoke it much better than I did. For that reason, and because of his greater experience in the field, we had decided that he should be the one to clear the way.

I saw him stop in front of the door of the right flat and rap it with his knuckles. We both knew that the inhabitant was a solitary man, the CIA had passed us that information, and that by silencing him no one else would disturb us in the building for as long as it took to carry out the task we'd been assigned.

After a few seconds the door opened inwards and through it peered the hard, weathered face of a man who looked to be in his forties. Tilson smiled weakly at him and held out his fake KGB badge with his left hand; when the man leaned forward to scrutinize it, he crushed his Adam's apple with an elbow.

We went in.

Tilson dragged the Russian's limp body and sat him on the floor, his back against a wall. Blood from his ruptured windpipe began to gush from his mouth and soak through the chest of the padded shirt he wore. Within seconds the man expired. He was not a civilian; he had belonged to the KGB border guard militia and was a loyal member of the Communist Party. That was why he'd been chosen; well, that and the privileged location of the flat where he lived.

While I stripped off my woolen coat and took the rifle parts out of their compartments, Tilson took cover near the window, which was in line with Major Kirov's office, and began to spy on him through a powerful pair of binoculars.

"That son of a bitch is punctual," he muttered in Russian. "How much longer are you going to take, kid? The sooner we finish the party, the better."

There's no denying I was annoyed to hear him call me "kid." I'd been codenamed Delta and I expected him to address me as such. But I guess to an old-timer like Tilson — Delta or not — I was just another rookie, and he probably felt responsible for me anyway.

I had already finished assembling the pieces of the rifle. I had done it in less time than usual because, as I have already explained, it was only the skeleton of the gun: the trigger mechanism with the bolt action, the scope, and the gun barrel. Something very similar to what actor Edward Fox had used to shoot General de Gaulle in the film *The Day of the Jackal.* So, it was no ordinary rifle, but one that had been altered by an expert gunsmith to meet the needs of our mission.

I tapped Tilson on one shoulder to let him know I was ready. The man looked me up and down, nodded his head and stepped back, giving me the space in front of the window.

I only had two cartridges with me, although one was supposed to suffice; they were hollow-point rounds. I took a position two feet away from the window — thus preventing anyone from seeing my silhouette in the skylight from the outside. I expelled all the air I had in my lungs; I would not breathe again until the shot was fired. I aligned the sight, which had already been adjusted beforehand, it would be a shot of three hundred and fifty meters across the square and with no wind to deflect the trajectory of the bullet. I focused on the window of Kirov's office and waited for its sole occupant to stand, as was his custom, before the skylight to watch the passers-by across Lubyanka Square, three floors below his level.

He had a thoughtful expression on his face as I began to pull the trigger very slowly, inexorably... until the rifle discharged.

One shot. One kill.

The second round was not necessary.

As it is logical to think, when his death became widely

known, many people around the globe wondered who did eliminate Kirov: A contract killer? A CIA enforcer, or perhaps a highly skilled MI6 operative? Or, maybe, it was his rivals within the KGB's Directorate S?

In short, the speculations were manifold, but the most knowledgeable in the international Intelligence community understood that the Quadrille had just sent a clear and categorical message to all our enemies around the world: *No one messes with America and gets away with it!*

THE END

ABOUT THE AUTHOR

OSCAR ORTIZ was born in 1959 (Matanzas, Cuba), but he was raised in the United States. From an early age he showed his vocation for art and literature and (to the same extent) his dislike for collective sports, business, science, and math. He spent his youth studying commercial art & advertising. Ortiz is the winner of the "Sole Second Prize" in the **2006 ENRIQUE LABRADOR RUIZ INTERNATIONAL STORYWRITERS AWARD** with his crime story *La culpa fue de Hammett* (Blame it on Hammett) and selected as "Finalist" in the **2006 TELEMUNDO WRITERS WORKSHOP** contest. He has worked as a freelance screenwriter for Telemundo Puerto Rico and Cubana de Televisión Studios in Miami. He currently resides with his wife in South Florida.